THE FINE ART OF
KEEPING QUIET

CHARITY TAHMASEB

Collins Mark Books

Copyright

To Kyra, who always knows what to say.

Speak the speech, I pray you, as I pronounced it to you, trippingly on the tongue

Hamlet, Act III, Scene II

Contents

Chapter 1

MY FEET ARE STUCK in a clump of snow at the bus stop, a haze of exhaust swirling around me. I need to get home so we can drive back to school for conferences—or speed-dating with teachers, as my mom calls it—where Mr. Henderson can tell my parents how I'm failing speech. You'd think that would be my biggest problem at the moment. Yeah. You'd think. But it's not.

Thing is, I'm really failing speech, the epic kind of failure that means repeating the class, maybe even summer school. I don't know what I'm going to do if that happens. I don't know what I'm going to do in half an hour when my parents sit down with Mr. Henderson. But right this second, I don't know how I'm going to walk past the rink rats.

The rink rats, as my brother Derek calls them, all skate in the youth hockey league and they practice in the park near my house. On most days, I wait them out. I stamp my feet and blow warm breath into damp mittens and let frost fringe my eyelashes until the rink rats move on. Eventually, they'll abandon the sidewalk in front of Meadow Park for the hockey rinks behind it.

But today, they stand there, in between my bus stop and home, skates slung over their shoulders and sticks in hand. They are armed, and dangerous, and once upon a time, before Derek went off to college, they weren't even an issue.

Wind stings my cheeks. My jacket feels thin, and I feel unprotected inside it. I tug my scarf up and over my mouth so its edge tickles the tip of my nose. Somehow, this feels safer. When another bus pulls up, I see my chance. I take a few steps, my boots crunching a mix of icy snow, sand, and salt. One of the rink rats heads for the warming hut, leaving the other two behind. *Yes!* Two against one isn't so bad. I take a few more steps. Head down, I'm a few feet away when I hear them.

"Hey, bro. Here comes your girlfriend." It's one of the rink rats, and he doesn't say *girlfriend* like it's a nice word.

"Are you sure?" This is Crandall. That's his last name. I only know this because it's on the back of his hockey jersey. If the rink rats were a wolf pack, Crandall would be their alpha. As if to prove my theory, the first rink rat howls. It's a sound that feels colder than the wind.

"Now I see her," Crandall says. "Hey, bay-bee."

The rink rats have always been mean. I'm sure that in preschool they pushed other kids down to get to the choicest Saltines. But in the last few months, their words scare me more, make my feet freeze in their tracks. When I inhale, my lungs hold icicles.

"Wanna go to the Valentine's dance?" Crandall says. "Of course, you'll have to wear a bag over your head."

"That's the only kind of date you could get." The other boy folds his arms across his chest and smirks at Crandall.

Who shoves the other first, I can't say, but a spark of hope warms my chest. If their fight goes on long enough, I can sneak past. They'll be too busy with each other to care about me. The soles of my boots squeak in the snow. I wince, hope they don't hear, and fight the temptation to run. Running is the worst thing you can do. It makes you look scared.

Wolves—and rink rats—love that.

"Hey, bay-bee, where you going?"

Part of me wants to spin around, shove him in the chest, and shout, "Hey, bay-bee, I have a name." But I don't say anything. Your name isn't something you give to a rink rat. Even Derek was careful never to use my name—Jolia—around them.

"Cut it out," someone says.

This isn't the other rink rat. It certainly isn't Crandall. I feel myself turn, almost like I'm being pulled by a thin, invisible wire.

The boy stands a few feet away, a new arrival from that other school bus. I know him. Or knew him. I'm not sure which. His name is Sam, and his eyes make me think of summer.

"Who do we have here?" Crandall says. "A boyfriend?" He doesn't say this like it's a nice word either.

The other rink rat snorts. "No way, dude. He's the one with the boyfriend."

Now, the word sounds even worse. Sam's face flushes pink, and Crandall laughs like this is the funniest joke ever.

From the top of the hill, a voice calls, "Hey, are we going to skate or what?" It's the third rink rat, back from the rink. I gulp a breath. If he starts down the hill, we really will be outnumbered.

Crandall glances toward the hill and back again, then his eyes narrow at Sam like he has ruined everything. And Sam? He takes a step forward.

I wait for the worst.

"This sucks, man," Crandall says at last. "Let's skate."

So they leave. Just like that. But of course, as he walks past, Crandall's shoulder knocks into mine. I stumble back only to have my elbow caught by Sam.

He frowns after them and mutters, "A-holes."

I try to speak, but it's like the rink rats have stolen all my words. My insides quake. My eyes are hot with unshed tears. Sam's bravery amazes me, and I wish I could tell him that.

"You okay?" he says.

I nod, then manage, "Yeah. Thanks." The words come out of my mouth with tiny puffs of fog.

"Do they do this all the time?" Sam asks.

I look away and he knows the answer.

"Maybe you should tell someone."

Yes, I know I should. Everyone says to do that: parents, teachers, pop stars on YouTube. Sure, my parents would listen, but both Sam and I know how it would go. The torment might stop—for a while. Then the rink rats would invent something new, something worse.

"Or maybe," he begins, and I catch the hint of a grin in his voice. "You could join a sport or something and take the activity bus home." He nods toward the park. "They'd be skating by then."

They'd be cutting up the ice and wouldn't risk ruining their skates just to mess with me.

"I might do that," I say.

"I usually take that bus," he adds, "but I have conferences today."

We don't go to the same school, never have. Sam might live in Fremont, Minnesota, like I do, but he's in the Winnetka school district. As long as I can remember, whatever our school did, Winnetka had to do it better, so it doesn't surprise me that they have conferences today, too.

"Well. See ya," he says. "I'm going to be late."

"Me too."

But we just stand there, like both of us want to say something. I haven't seen him up close since the summer before seventh grade. He's taller now, taller than I am. Dark bangs peek from beneath a knit cap. His eyes remind me of all the summers we spent together, right here, in Meadow Park. Their color is the glimpse of blue between the green and brown of the largest oak. Summer green, I think, and they stare at me now as if something intrigues him.

But he doesn't mention those days. I wonder if he even remembers me and how we played until the mosquitoes chased us home, how he was my summer best friend. Instead, he jerks, something that starts as a wave, but ends as a swipe at his bangs. Then he turns and walks toward his house.

I wave, but his back is turned and he doesn't see me. I trudge home, wondering why the idea of Sam forgetting our summers feels worse, in some ways, than failing speech.

———————

"I DON'T UNDERSTAND. I simply don't understand."

My mom has said this a dozen times, at least, during the conference. She started on a fresh round before we even sat down in Mr. Henderson's classroom. My dad is here and so is the guidance counselor, Ms. Patel.

This is special. This is serious. This isn't your normal school conference.

"How can Jolia be doing so well—straight As—in all her classes but one?" Mom asks.

That's the million dollar question. I wish I had an answer. So must everyone else, because for a long time, no one says anything. I begin to feel like I do during speech class itself, my insides like ice, hoping (usually beyond hope) that Mr. Henderson won't call on me.

My mouth feels awkward, like my teeth are too large for my jaw. I press my fingers against my upper lip. No braces. Not anymore. My teeth are straight. Sometimes that's hard to believe without a mirror.

Mom reaches over and gently tugs my wrist so my hand slips

away from my mouth and into my lap. Her fingers are cool. They don't tremble, but I know she's nervous.

"I'm going to outline a few options that Jolia has at this point," Mr. Henderson says, clearing his throat. He pauses to make sure he has everyone's attention. My parents lean forward, and even Ms. Patel props her chin on her hand.

"One option is Jolia can make up the speeches she's missed plus give a handful of extra-credit speeches before the end of the term."

I feel my eyes go wide at the prospect of writing and giving that many speeches. Apparently, Mr. Henderson doesn't think much of this option, because he continues.

"Or, perhaps it would be best if Jolia drops speech and retakes it during the last term."

"What?" comes out of my mouth before I can stop it. "But I have creative storytelling." Fear forces the words from me. The honors elective is by application only. Mrs. Riley has already approved the outline for the graphic novel my best friend Caro and I plan to write. We're the only sophomores in the course this year. And if I drop it? I doubt Mrs. Riley will give me another chance to take it.

Mr. Henderson's expression is bland. He narrows his eyes at me, like the last thing I should worry about is my graphic novel. Maybe he's right. Creative storytelling isn't a blow-off elective, but without speech, I can't graduate.

Dad coughs. "That's an option," he says, "but I'd hate to see Jolia miss out on creative storytelling."

"Actions have consequences," Mr. Henderson says.

Or in my case, non-actions, because, in truth, the only thing I haven't done in speech is talk. Just because during last week's speech, I froze in front of everyone and then just stood there— mute, for three whole minutes—doesn't mean I should fail speech.

Okay, maybe it does.

Dad bristles, and I know he's going to say something, something that will probably land me in summer school, or worse.

"Actually," Ms. Patel says before Dad can speak, "I'm not entirely certain Jolia can stay in the honors program if she drops speech this term."

An urge to bolt from the room washes over me. Mom must feel it, too, because she clutches my hand. I'm not certain if she's keeping me here or the other way around. With one sentence, Ms. Patel has sent my future plans crashing, like one domino into another. No honors program? No chance at a scholarship. No scholarship? I don't know what that means. But things are tight with Derek at college—and he has scholarships.

"May I?" Ms. Patel leans forward and studies the screen on Mr. Henderson's laptop. "Hmm ... interesting. Jolia has turned in all her written assignments on time."

Mom and Dad exchange looks. Mr. Henderson glances toward the ceiling.

"And for one hundred percent credit as well," Ms. Patel continues. "It seems Jolia has a grasp on how to outline a speech, and how to write in general, wouldn't you say, Mr. Henderson?"

He nods like this fact pains him.

"And her grades in American Literature reflect that. So, really, what she needs to work on is the performance aspect, actually standing up in front of a group and speaking. Am I right?"

Mr. Henderson's face is blank, and he gives one stiff nod. Mom edges closer to Ms. Patel and the laptop. Ms. Patel shifts so Mom can see my grades.

"What about a third option?" Ms. Patel says.

"For instance?" Both Dad and Mr. Henderson say at once.

"For instance." Ms. Patel points to the poster on the wall behind Mr. Henderson's desk. It says *The Fremont Free Speakers Want You!*

"Weren't you saying," she adds, her question directed at Mr. Henderson. "That the team needs more members?"

Mr. Henderson looks like he's going to choke on his own spit. Yes, the team is recruiting—hard. They lost all their award-winning seniors from last year. The co-captain twins, Ryan and Tory Dinsmore, have plastered posters all over school and they even did a funny routine at the last pep rally. But Mr. Henderson probably wants members of the Fremont Free Speakers with the ability to speak freely.

"It's perfect for a case like Jolia's," Ms. Patel says. "She'll attend practice during the week, and all the tournaments are on Saturdays …"

Tournaments? How much better is that than repeating speech class? My palms start to sweat. "Every Saturday?" I squeak.

"Here." Ms. Patel hands me a sheet of paper from Mr. Henderson's desk. I count nine tournaments between now and April.

"I'm not really sure this addresses the problem," Mr. Henderson begins.

Everyone knows the speech team is his pride and joy. Last year, eight team members went to state, and four to national. Why ruin a record like that with me? I don't blame him for hating this idea. I don't like it much myself.

"How about a trial basis?" Ms. Patel suggests. "Jolia doesn't need another term of learning how to write a speech. What she needs is a little help overcoming her performance anxiety. What if she continues in speech class and uses her participation on the team to raise her grade?"

The silence in the room falls cold and hard. I don't dare breathe, and I don't think my parents do either.

"Practice is every day after school," Mr. Henderson says. "Attendance is mandatory on Tuesdays. Although to prove you're serious and to *improve*, I'd expect to see you every day." This last sounds more like he's insisting I eat a big plate of liver and onions. It sounds like he's hoping I refuse.

"Practice?" My voice wavers on that word. Eating a big plate of liver sounds so much better than speaking in front of a group every day after school.

Mr. Henderson scowls. "Will that be a problem?"

Before Dad can jump in, Ms. Patel adds, "If transportation is an issue, there's always the activity bus. Practice will end in time for her to catch the last one, won't it, Mr. Henderson?" Ms. Patel beams at him. Oh, she's good.

"Yes." Mr. Henderson sighs. "It does."

I hear an echo of Sam in my head. *After school ... activity bus.* I think of the walk home, the way clear of rink rats. I wonder if the Winnetka activity bus drops off at the same time. I wonder if Sam will be on that bus. There's enough wonder in these thoughts that it makes speech team seem almost bearable.

Everyone is staring at me, so I raise my chin and say:

"I'll do it."

Chapter 2

EVERYONE KNOWS the cafeteria is the worst place to have a conversation. With all the noise, the scraping of chair legs against the floor, and the weird (and kind of disturbing) sounds coming from the back where the dishwashing machines are, talking isn't much of an option.

But shouting is. It's what Jeremy Spinner is doing now, hands cupped around his mouth. His words fly past my best friend Caro and me and somehow reach the boys sitting at the table across from ours.

"Boo-ya!" one of the boys yells back, although I'm pretty sure he doesn't know what Jeremy said. How could he? I don't know what Jeremy said. But then, I don't pay a lot of attention to him.

That's Caro's job. Ever since they started going together at the beginning of the school year, a big part of Caro's day revolves around paying attention to Jeremy. I don't know if it's boys in general, or Jeremy in particular, but he seems to need a lot of it.

"I talked my mom into picking me up late today," Caro says to me now. "I told her we were doing a project, but we can watch the first part of Jeremy's basketball practice."

Yes, Jeremy's a jock. There's never a season he isn't in at least one school sport and some traveling team on the weekends. Caro would like to go to all his games but she isn't allowed to date until she's sixteen, and then, there are rules for that.

Of course, now Caro's breaking all those rules—and I've been helping her. Sometimes something pings inside me, like what I'm doing isn't quite right. But I'm not sure it's wrong, either. According to Caro, everyone in tenth grade is dating, which isn't exactly true. I'm not dating. Her point is, I could if I wanted to—and if anyone asked.

But Caro is my best friend, and I'd do anything for her. But today is Monday, the first day of speech team practice. I can't skip that for basketball, or a ride home, or even Caro.

"I can't." I say this to my lunch tray, as if I'm merely betraying the French toast sticks and not my best friend.

Caro gives her head a little shake, her eyes clouded with confusion. I know her schedule by heart, and she knows mine. This isn't on the agenda because I haven't told Caro I'm joining the speech team.

I haven't told her I'm failing speech.

"Speech team practice," I say.

"Speech team practice?" Caro's voice pitches an octave higher. "Since when? You hate speaking in front of people."

She knows me that well. Even after a full weekend of thinking up excuses, I still don't have a good one. I can't confess here, not in front of Jeremy and the rowdy jocks at the next table, all spilt milk and spilt dreams.

"I ... thought I'd try it," I say at last. "Mr. Henderson says I can get extra credit."

Caro squints at me, like she doesn't believe me. Why should

she? I don't believe me. She grabs my wrist and then turns to Jeremy.

"We have to go to the bathroom. Can you take care of our stuff?" She waves a hand at our discarded lunch trays.

"Sure, babe." Jeremy swivels and starts shouting at the boys at the other table. I'm sure our lunch trays will still be there when the bell rings for next block.

In the bathroom Caro does a stall check, shoving each door open, and sings out, "Anyone home?" Her hair gleams in the light. Caro's curls are high maintenance but totally worth it. She slathers on every product you can buy at Target just to keep them fashion magazine glossy. Between that, her dusky skin, and eyelashes that need no mascara, she's the prettiest girl in tenth grade, maybe the whole school—something all the boys noticed this fall.

Of course, after winter break, no one noticed I'd gotten my braces off—not even Caro. Now, in the bathroom, I try to ignore my reflection—my chin length hair, super straight without a curl in sight. At least now my teeth match.

Caro whirls and stares me down, arms crossed over her chest. "What's going on?"

"I—" My voice deserts me. It's speech class all over again, words frozen in my throat, my mouth feeling all awkward and weird. I channel all my thoughts into one wish: *Please remember.*

I know she does, up to a point. In fact, back in grade school, I used to make her laugh by doing chipmunk impressions. But when you're ten, big front teeth are kind of cute and funny. It seemed like they kept getting larger, until I almost couldn't press my lips together.

"Her mouth is just too small to handle all of these teeth," the orthodontist had told my parents. I'd never been self-conscious about how I looked before. Overnight, I went from being the girl with the cute chipmunk teeth to donkey girl. The orthodontist tried a few things—tooth extraction, for one—to see if my teeth would sort themselves out. They didn't. So my braces went on just as everybody else's were coming off—or so it seemed.

The first day I walked into school after getting braces, my whole head ached, from my jaw to the top of my skull. I tried to keep my mouth closed, my braces hidden, but girls kept noticing, first one, then the other until at lunch, everybody wanted to see.

"Wow, your teeth are really crooked," one girl said.

"It's why I got braces," I mumbled.

Caro leaned across me and got in the girl's face. "Wow, thanks Captain Obvious. You should be a detective," she said, then waved her hands in the air, silencing everyone. "Viewing hours are over."

That put a stop to it. Almost. Later, in the bathroom, I heard two girls talking, whispering like they were afraid Caro could hear them all the way in the cafeteria.

"Her teeth are so ... I don't know what. I'm glad that's not me."

"Seriously. Can you even imagine anyone wanting to kiss that?"

"Ew, what if he, like, got his tongue stuck or something."

"I can't remember why I ever thought she was pretty."

I hid in a stall until they left. I never told Caro.

That afternoon, I froze in front of class. Caro and I were doing a presentation on the War of 1812 for social studies. I opened my mouth to speak and nothing came out. My upper lip felt weird, like my front two teeth were pressing against it. At any moment, they would burst through, ugly and crooked.

I pressed my fingertips against my mouth, desperate to push my teeth back inside. My braces dug into my lips. I couldn't speak, couldn't remove the hand from in front of my face. At last, Caro gave me the laser pointer and read my part of the presentation.

When we were back at our seats, she leaned over, her face worried. "Does your mouth still hurt?" she whispered.

That was it! Relief ran through me, and I nodded.

Except that wasn't it. Every time the urge to speak up hit me, soft, insidious whispers filled my head.

Can you even imagine anyone wanting to kiss that ... his tongue stuck or something ... can't remember why I ever thought she was pretty.

Over the next few years, I'd perfected the art of keeping quiet: whether it was for a group presentation or reading out loud, I found a way not to open my mouth. Until I slammed into speech class, it had worked, too.

Now Caro studies me. Her eyes radiate doubt, her hair a little frizzy from our flight through the cafeteria. "Speech team?" she says. "Really?"

My teeth threaten to sprout through my upper lip. I resist the urge to check my reflection in the mirror. The braces have been off for weeks, my new teeth polished and shiny. But like someone who has lost a limb, I can still feel how they used to be, how they crowded my mouth and made it impossible to speak.

Telling Caro this is a lot like admitting I'm ugly. Not in an "Ugh, I look awful" kind of way, but deep down ugly, like there's something wrong with me that can never be fixed. And who wants a broken best friend?

"I really could use the extra credit," I manage at last. That, I tell myself, is not a lie. Not really. I start to say more, but Caro interrupts me.

"I guess it kind of sucks to have to do something you really, really hate."

I let out a breath. Yeah. It really does.

———

I STAND in the doorway of the speech team room—not all the way in, not all the way out. My stomach is tied into a bunch of little knots, each one sharp and stabbing. My palms are sweaty, but really, at this point, that's minor.

I take in the Fremont Free Speakers. I know most of them. Some are in pre-calculus with me. Others are in my Honors American Literature class. But when one starts to stare, they all do. I'm not a total stranger to school activities. I play violin in the orchestra, and I'm vice president of the knitting club. But this?

"Are you joining speech?" Co-captain Ryan Dinsmore calls from the back of the room. He's lounging across two desks like he owns the place.

I nod.

Disbelief crosses his face. "Do you even talk?"

Everyone laughs. My head buzzes. I don't belong here. And they know it.

Mr. Henderson appears at the door and forces me inside the room. He welcomes everyone to a new season and goes on to introduce all the members. This takes less than a minute. Ryan Dinsmore might be all lazy and cavalier in the back of the room, but his brow crinkles. Despite the recruiting effort, the team is small.

I'm taking notes about the available PowerPoints on the team website (polished presentations, dress for success, tournament etiquette) when co-captain Tory Dinsmore blows into the room. In grade school, kids called her Tornado. Behind her back, some still do. She levels a look at her twin, Ryan. He jerks up, soles of his sneakers slapping the floor. Then, Tory takes the rest of us in.

Her eyes say it all: we are puny and unworthy of her speech team. I can't say how I know this. I just do. Probably the same way I instantly know that despite sharing the team co-captain slot with her brother, it's Tory who's in charge.

"Tory, so glad you made it," Mr. Henderson says without a trace of sarcasm.

"Sorry," Tory says. "I had to catch the bus back from Fremont State."

Next to me, two freshmen raise eyebrows at each other. Yes, Tory wants all of us to know she's taking college classes already. I refrain from rolling my eyes.

"This is a student-led, student-run team," Mr. Henderson says. "I'm here for consultation and critique, but now that we have both co-captains, I'll leave you to it." He spreads his arms wide, encompassing the whole room, then retreats to his desk in the back.

Tory gives us a huge grin. "Welcome to the Fremont Free Speakers!"

For one awful moment, I think we're in for a repeat of Mr. Henderson's introductions, but apparently Tory doesn't need such things.

"Ryan," she says, digging through her messenger bag. "Take the returning members and go over the strength-weakness matrix and work on event and piece selection." She hands Ryan a stack of papers. "Think strategic. Think beating Winnetka. Think State."

"It's a lock," Ryan says. He's the lazy river to her whirlwind of activity. He pushes himself from the desk like this is the most difficult thing he's done all day and heads to one corner of the room.

"Okay, newbies." Tory drags a chair to the white board in the front of the room. "Once you understand the events, we can get into the fun stuff, like piece selection and refinement. But first, I gotta show you this." From her messenger bag, she pulls out a digital video camera.

"Christmas present," she sings. "Ryan got one, too. Sure, there's the team equipment." She waves a hand toward the back of the room, acknowledging and dismissing the equipment all at once. "But this is better. Now we can spot-critique on the fly, catch you from two angles at once. Everyone will get plenty of chances to record their piece."

As in speaking into the camera? I'm pretty sure I have something to say about that. But my throat goes tight. Any words I might have are stuck. A croak emerges, not from me, but from the boy one seat over.

"Recording our pieces?" he asks, his voice cracking on the last word. He's a junior named Ben, and he's in my pre-calculus class.

"It's the best way to improve your performance." Tory leans forward and clutches the camera like it's made of gold. "It's like magic."

Tory talks us through the two overall events: public speaking and interpretive. Public speaking is about speeches of all kinds: your own, someone else's, pulling a topic and writing a speech at each tournament. Interpretive is poetry and storytelling and drama. You pick a piece and perform it all season long. I know all this. I did some research over the weekend and asked Mr. Henderson during class if I could use serious prose as my category.

"I suppose that's up to you and the team captains," was all he said.

Tory lists each event up on the white board. "During the first week or two, you can change your mind, and of course we'll want to leverage strengths, but let's see who's interested in what."

By the show of hands, it's clear. Every last one of us wants serious prose, poetry, or drama.

"What?" Tory widens her eyes in what must be mock astonishment. "No one wants extemporaneous speaking?"

"Ex … tem … who?" Ben says. Tiny drops of sweat sprinkle his brow. He's a wrestler and isn't someone I'd expect to see on the speech team. He casts me a look, and I wonder if somehow his reasons mirror my own.

"Each time you go to a tournament," Tory says, her voice patient. "You'll draw a topic—usually something about current events. Then you write and present your speech. It's so invigorating!"

"So's getting your face washed in a snow bank," Ben whispers. "You don't see me signing up for *that*."

"I will personally coach anyone who signs up for extemporaneous speaking."

"Sure," Ben mutters. "Like that clinches the deal."

I snort a laugh. Tory glares at us through half-lidded eyes. We are unworthy. Again.

"Okay, okay. It's a little intimidating at first," she concedes. "But if you're doing any of the interpretative categories, piece selection is key. You simply can't pull something you read in the American Lit textbook and call it done. The piece needs to be fresh but not off the wall. If it's new, it's got to have some literary street cred. If it's a classic, it can't be run into the ground. Plus, it should fit your personality."

I inch my book bag closer. Part of my weekend research included finding the perfect piece. I even typed the scene I wanted to do into my laptop and formatted it the way the speech team handbook said to. Now, while I sit facing Tory, my hand ransacks the contents of my book bag until my fingers find the folder with my piece.

"For example," Tory says. "Every year, half the new kids in the prose category do something from *Flowers for Algernon*." Here, Tory pauses to stick her finger down her throat like she's gagging. "Nothing will mark you as a noob faster than that. Same goes for anything from the American Lit text."

My hand freezes on the folder, my heart thumping hard and sharp.

"I'm saying it now: There will be no *Algernon* on the Fremont Free Speakers. Got that?"

I shove the folder with my piece—the one I had so carefully copied from *Flowers for Algernon*—back into my bag.

"Anyone have a piece picked out yet? Anyone?" Tory looks around.

The freshmen slouch in their seats. Next to me, Ben tucks a battered copy of the American Lit text beneath his sweatshirt.

"Jolia, how about you?" Tory asks.

I'm caught in her blue-eyed gaze, like an animal trapped in

headlights, my hand still stuck in my book bag. At last, I go with the truth. "Well, I had this scene from *Flowers for Algernon* ..."

Ben bursts out laughing; even the freshmen giggle. From across the room, Ryan snickers. Tory stares at me hard, like she knows what I said isn't a joke. I want to sink into my seat or run to the bathroom to check my teeth. I can't do either, so I stare back and take in the full force of Tory's message:

I am not worthy.

Chapter 3

IN LESS THAN A WEEK, I will speak at my first tournament. I will stand in front of judges and students for eight minutes. For those eight minutes, words will have to come from my mouth. I'll have to do that three times.

Three times eight is twenty four. Twenty four minutes of speaking. Just me. Caro can't save me; I know Tory won't. My stomach clenches every time I think about it.

So I try not to. Instead, I think about my other problem: finding eight minutes worth of words. I've paged through dozens of books, read so many short stories that my eyes are starting to cross. The words all blur into each other. I search the National Book Award and Printz Honor lists, looking for the perfect title, but nothing feels right. I'll have to live with this piece for the entire season. It's not exactly like picking a best friend, but I can't help thinking of it that way.

Tonight I'm ready to give up. It's Sunday and I must have a final piece selected by tomorrow at speech team practice. I've picked so many for Mr. Henderson's approval that even if I do find the perfect piece, I'm not sure he'll take me seriously.

Instead of searching, I grab one of my favorite books from the shelf. Five minutes, I tell myself, then I'll go back to looking.

Twenty minutes later, Mom pokes her head into my room.

"Reading?" she asks.

I eye the book in my hands but don't say anything since the answer is pretty obvious.

Mom laughs as if she knows it was a silly question. "Homework done?"

I nod.

"Visiting old friends?"

I glance at the copy of *Jane Eyre* and nod again.

"It's one of my favorites." Mom gets a dreamy look, and for a second I'm afraid she might snatch the book away from me, dash off to the living room, and read it herself.

She doesn't. Instead, she says, "What's funny is I've always liked the first part of the book better, before Jane meets Mr. Rochester." Mom shrugs. "He's kind of a jerk."

"That's one word for it," I say, but an idea tickles the back of my mind, and I grip the book tighter.

"Don't stay up too late reading."

"I won't."

Mom blows a kiss and turns to leave.

I wait until her footsteps fade, then I sit up straight in bed. Just like Mom, my favorite part is BR—before Rochester. I page to a passage I think might work, the one where Jane has just been sent to that horrid boarding school. The superintendent, Mr. Brockle-hurst, calls her a liar and makes her stand on a stool, in front of everyone, for hours.

Really, could a speech tournament be any worse? I doubt it. Besides, why not read something I love? That way, no matter how awful the tournaments are, I'll always have this one thing. I may not be worthy, but something tells me *Jane Eyre* is.

———

MONDAY AFTERNOON at speech practice the only thing that keeps me running from the room is my copy of *Jane Eyre* clutched in my hands. One of the other prose girls, Savannah, wanted to look at it, and I seriously could not pry it from my grip. I can't let it go. I can't approach Mr. Henderson either. He's sitting at his desk in the back of the room.

I need his permission to perform *Jane Eyre* in the tournaments. I wait and I wait, but Ryan is lounging across the back desks again, and Mr. Henderson hasn't budged from his own. I don't want an audience for this, but since practice is half over, I don't have much of a choice.

I inch forward, hoping Ryan will decide to move—or Tory will decide for him. I scoot past, still hoping, but he peers at me, one eye covered by a fringe of blond bangs. He looks like a refugee from a boy band.

"Mr. Henderson?" My voice is all froggy, so I clear my throat and try again. "Mr. Henderson?"

He glances up. I think he sighs. I am probably the last person he wants to see.

"Yes, Jolia?" he says.

"I was wondering if I could change my piece, you see—"

"Seriously?" Ryan. He has his head tipped back and is giving us an upside down stare. "You change pieces like I change my underwear."

My thoughts explode with sudden anger. This isn't any of his business.

"Well, that's not saying much," flies from my mouth before I can think twice.

22

Ryan's eyes go big, like he can't believe I said that, but Mr. Henderson looks like he hasn't even heard us. Instead, he says, "So, you want to change your piece." He doesn't add *again*, but I hear it in his voice.

"It's from *Jane Eyre*," I tell him. "This is the last time, I promise."

"The scene when Jane and Rochester meet?" Mr. Henderson asks.

I shake my head. "No, when Jane is at boarding school and Mr. Brocklehurst makes her stand on that stool."

Mr. Henderson doesn't say a word, but he holds out his hand. I pry the book from my grip and open it to the bookmarked page.

"I thought I'd write an introduction about schools and bullying —a compare and contrast." I tell him. "How some things change, and some things don't."

"Interesting," he says, flipping through the pages.

Interesting doesn't mean *no*, so I hold my breath. Mr. Henderson still hasn't said anything when Ryan pipes up.

"Isn't *Jane Eyre* a chick book?" he says.

Mr. Henderson's eyes narrow, but his gaze lands on Ryan. "It would do you good to read more, Mr. Dinsmore." Mr. Henderson turns to me. "A suitable selection. Let's see how you do with it." He hands me the book.

I know better than to stay and hang around. Ryan does that and look at all the trouble he gets into. But as I pass his desk, I can't resist leaning down and whispering.

"Looks like you'll have to change your underwear."

———

"PASTELS ARE FOR WIMPS."

It's the first thing Tory says about my new piece. We back our scripts with construction paper. That way, when our fingers tremble or hands shake (and they will—at least, I know mine will), the thin computer paper won't rattle and distract the audience.

I went with a delicate light green because it reminded me of spring. Last night, I typed up everything and even wrote the introduction.

"You want to make a strong statement," Tory says now. "Pick a strong color."

I nod.

"Is this final?" she asks.

I nod again.

"Clear it with Henderson?"

"I did," I say.

Tory almost looks like she doesn't believe me. "What is it?"

"From *Jane Eyre*, the scene—"

She groans. "Don't tell me, the scene where they first meet, blah, blah, blah."

"No," I say, slowly, wondering what on earth *Jane Eyre*—or that scene—ever did to anyone. "It's the scene when Jane is at Lowood, and the superintendent has her stand on the stool in front of the whole school and talks about how awful she is."

A spark lights Tory's face. It almost looks like approval. "Oh, excellent. I don't think I've heard anyone do that before. And it's perfect for you, since you're so ..." She trails off, then seems to give herself a mental shake. "Let's go over the text," she continues. "*Jane Eyre* has a lot of description, and you're allowed to cut things out for the most dramatic reading."

I'm so *what*, I wonder, but I don't question Tory or refuse her help. In half an hour, she even has me in front of the digital camera, where I manage to flub every single line in my script.

Even if I can't read the piece, I know it's the right one. I'd like to think if Jane Eyre were in tenth grade, she might play the violin and be vice president of the knitting club. She might have a beautiful best friend. She might be *my* friend. As I stand there, holding my script, I start to think that maybe she is.

I AM NOT READY. I am so not ready. Tory and Mr. Henderson have worked with all the new members, but with the exception of Kaitlin, who's doing poetry, we all stumble through our pieces. Tory cuts the digital camera practices short because the camera really does add ten pounds—of horrible.

It's Friday and I can't believe a week has zipped by. I can't believe it's February already. I can't believe tomorrow I'll be attending my first speech tournament. I go through the line at lunch, then realize what a waste of money that is—I can't eat a thing.

"Nervous?" Caro asks when I sit at our table.

I squeeze my eyes shut and nod.

"Then here." Caro places a tiny white box on the table in front of me.

"What is this?"

"Open it and find out."

So I do. Inside, on a bed of cotton, is a charm for my half of our BFF necklace. I turn the tiny megaphone with my fingertips. The silvery surface is smooth and cool. It's pretty, but it doesn't make any sense. I never worry about sounding rude with Caro, so the question pops out of my mouth.

"Megaphone?"

"Because you're speaking tomorrow," she says, as if that explains it all.

"Isn't this for cheerleading?"

"Words come out of them," Caro says, pointing to the mega-phone. "Words come out of your mouth." Her finger moves from the megaphone in my palm to my mouth. "It's so the world can hear you."

I'm not sure I want the world—or anyone—to hear me. The donkey teeth feel as though they've really sprouted through my upper lip. At the same time, hot tears sting my eyes. Caro has been my best friend since I helped her find her missing milk stick on the first day of kindergarten—no stick, no milk (but thinking back, I'm sure sweet Mrs. Pederson would've let Caro have milk, stick or no).

That's why I'm doing this, standing up in front of strangers and enduring twenty four minutes of speaking. So next term, she can draw the pictures, and I can fill in the words, and for one class, it will be just us, BFFs—the way it used to be.

———

THAT AFTERNOON, I walk into speech team practice expecting a tornado, the sort that Tory whips up—both cameras running, everyone making last minute fixes to their performances, everyone talking over everyone else.

Instead, the entire team is circled around Ryan and his laptop. No one speaks above a whisper. I glance around for Mr. Henderson, but he isn't here. So I move closer to see what's caught everyone's attention.

"Click refresh again," Tory says. "They always update the roster on Friday afternoon."

I hear a click, then a gasp. "There it is!" Tory says. "Come on, load faster."

I'm close enough now to peer over her shoulder. I can see the top half of Ryan's laptop screen. He has a web browser open, and on top of the page, it says: *Winnetka High School Speech Team.*

"Are we spying?" I ask, my voice a whisper.

"Not really," Tory says. "Every Friday, Winnetka updates their tournament roster."

"On the members-only part of the site?" I ask.

The room goes even quieter, although I'm not sure how that's possible. "Are we supposed to be doing this?" I add.

"Oh, sure." Ryan glances at me through his bangs. "Now you decide to talk."

I ignore him. "Don't we update our roster?"

Tory nods.

I imagine a group of kids over at Winnetka High School, huddled around a laptop, having this exact same conversation. We hack their site; they hack ours. If that's the case, I'm not sure how any of this matters. But Tory's jaw is clenched, and Ryan has his fingers crossed.

"Not discussion, not discussion, not discussion," he mutters. Then, "Yes! Romero isn't doing discussion." Ryan slumps in his chair.

"Maybe you'll have a chance this year," Tory says.

Ryan makes a face, and the two freshmen girls, Kaitlin and Savannah, giggle. They both have a crush on him. I hate to be the one to tell them, but he just doesn't change his underwear all that often. I laugh at this, which is stupid, because now everyone is staring at me.

"Who's Romero?" I say, to divert attention.

"Romeo Romero." Tory plants a hand on her hip. "Also known as Ryan's nemesis in discussion."

"Nem ... a ... who?" This, of course, is Ben.

Tory rolls her eyes. "Archrival. Moriarty to his Sherlock Holmes."

Ben stares blankly.

"Like Plankton and Mr. Krabs," she says.

"Oh ..." echoes around the room.

Tory shakes her head. We are still unworthy.

Ryan mouths a few words I'm glad I can't hear.

"He also went to state last year in prose," Tory adds. "He didn't place, but he came close."

"He's only a sophomore, too," Ryan says. "But he's already one of their stars." He sounds disgusted by this.

Tory nods, but when Savannah whispers, "He's cute," Tory points a finger at her.

"Cute enough to steal everything right out from under us," Tory says. "I swear, if their coach could, she'd put him in every single category. He's that good."

"He's in two this tournament," Ryan says. "Serious prose and humorous interpretation."

"Crap." Tory surveys us, her eyes narrow, and her mouth a thin, hard line. "Why don't we have anyone who's funny?"

"Or anyone who's serious," Ryan quips.

"But ... but," Savannah says, "I'm in prose, and so is Jolia."

Yes, and unfortunately, her reading of *To Kill a Mockingbird* is only slightly better than my *Jane Eyre*. The room goes silent. Even if I could say something in my defense (and I can't), the donkey teeth won't let me. My mouth feels clumsy and stupid. The best thing to do is say nothing at all, which is what the entire team decides to do. Savannah's words hang in the air for several awful moments until Tory clears her throat.

"It could be a ruse," she says before pointing at both me and Savannah. "You two, your mission is to watch out for him in prose, whether in one of your rounds or the finals." Tory's eyes meet Ryan's. For that moment, they're united. "We can have someone sit in on the humorous interp finals."

Ben snorts. "How can you know he'll make the finals?"

Tory and Ryan exchange that look again. "Oh, we know," they both say.

"Why do they call him Romeo?" Savannah asks.

A sly smile lights Tory's face. "Oh, you'll see," is all she says.

Chapter 4

SATURDAY MORNING ON THE BUS, I clutch my mittened hands together and try not to shake. Everyone around me has a case of jitters. Papers and note cards scatter across the floor, soaking up the puddles left from the dirty snow that clings to our good shoes. The ride to our first tournament at Worthington High School is way too short.

All the teams gather in the cafeteria, each school with its own table, except for Winnetka, which has commandeered three entire tables. Ben halts and the rest of us crash into him.

"Whoa. How many people do they have?" he asks.

"About thirty," Tory says, although how she forces the words through her clenched jaw, I'm not sure.

"Kind of like David and Goliath," I say.

Tory throws me a look that might be gratitude.

"David and who?" This is Ben. Of course.

"Rebel alliance versus the Death Star," I explain.

And now, Tory grins.

At our own table, we peel off jackets and see that everyone's good shoes match their nice outfits—mostly. Ben is anchored down by what must be his dad's tie. He catches my stare and shrugs.

Tory flings off her long wool coat to reveal the perfect debater's outfit, a serious suit in a blue so dark, it looks like midnight. Her blond hair is pulled back in a bun, and she wears glasses—not that she needs them.

"Okay, rookies," she says to us. "Let's go over this one more time."

I try to listen. I really do. Tory's an excellent speaker and makes dull things sound fascinating, even if she's only reciting what's in the speech team handbook. No matter how good—or bad—you happen to be, you will speak in three rounds. This is mandatory. Those with tops scores move onto the final round. Most kids pick a single category and piece and stick with it for the entire season. Kids like Tory and Ryan? Well, they're good enough to perform in two categories and take trophies home in both.

The noise in the cafeteria swallows Tory's voice. Conversations float around me, and my mind strays, my ears pricking at enticing words that have nothing to do with what Tory is talking about.

"Three rounds," Tory is saying. "After the third, there's a break. Eat your lunch, but don't get too sloppy. If you make it to the finals, the last thing you want is to be wearing ketchup."

Everyone laughs, but it sounds forced, like we're pushing the sound from our throats.

Tory continues, telling us how and when the scores are posted and where to check the finalist list. We're judged on a scale of one through five, with one being the best. You can't score lower than a five, even if there are more than five kids in your round. This, I think, is a good thing.

"Always check," she says. "Just because you think you tanked doesn't mean you did. And if you miss the finals …" She lets the sentence trail, but we all hear the unspoken threat despite the noise in the cafeteria.

Then a name catches my attention, and Tory's voice fades.

"Did you see who's back this year?" a girl says. She's standing close and I hear the squeal in her voice. "Sam Romero!"

"Romeo Romero? Lead me to him," a second girl says. "I'll be his Juliet."

My ears perk up at the name Sam. My Sam from the park, maybe? Okay, so he isn't *my* Sam. Still, I rack my brain, searching my memories. Does his last name start with an R? I scoot my chair closer, hoping for more clues.

"The Winnetka coach wants him at state this year," the first girl says. "He won't have time for any of us."

Sam. Winnetka. Coincidence? My mouth goes dry. Something deep inside insists this state-tourney bound Sam must be my Sam, but I can't bring myself to truly believe it.

"Excuse me, Jolia?" Tory's words have an edge sharp enough to cut. "Is this boring for you?" All of her earlier gratitude has evaporated.

I shake my head, my cheeks hot, but whether that's from Tory's scowl or the fact Sam might be somewhere in this school right now, I don't know.

———

I'M THINKING about getting new deodorant. A few weeks back, Mom bought me some vanilla chai scented kind. At first, I thought it was kind of cool. But now, waiting for the first round to start, sweat blooming all over my body, I worry that I smell like a Starbucks.

I sit in a strange classroom, my piece resting on the desk in front of me, the clock ticking down the seconds, while the judge at the back of the room sorts his critique sheets. Not only must I speak three times in front of total strangers today, three strange adults get to tell me how awful I am at it. When you think about it, it's kind of like a literary reality TV show. Add in Tory's nonstop cameras at practice, and it really is.

Failing speech doesn't sound so bad at the moment.

The judge asks the last student who enters to shut the classroom door, and it's like all the air is sucked out when she does.

"Welcome to the Worthington Speech Invitational," the judge says. "I'm Mr. Larson. I teach science here at Worthington High, but I participated in speech growing up. I like to revisit those days, this time on the other side."

A few giggles echo in the room, but I think most of us are too on edge to laugh.

"I won't tell you not to be nervous," he says, "because I always was. But remember, you're doing this for fun."

I have so many reasons for doing this. Fun hasn't made the top ten. But when I glance over my shoulder and see Mr. Larson give the whole room a smile, I wonder if it won't be that bad.

"First up." Mr. Larson peers at his list. "F-13, Jolia Cuppernull."

Okay, so it will be that bad.

I scoop up my script. Last night, I backed the pages with a dark forest green—oak leaf green. This color makes me think of summer, which reminds me of Sam. He's the last thing I should think about as I walk to the front of the room. For a few seconds, I'm not sure how to start. I'm not sure I'm supposed to start. Mr. Larson nods at me.

"Go on," he says. "I'll start your time ... now."

For a few more seconds, I do nothing but stand in front of the room. The phantom donkey teeth press behind my upper lip. If they grow too large, will I be able to talk around them? Will I be able to talk at all?

Mr. Larson nods again, and this time a slight frown appears above the wire-rimmed glasses he wears.

Fear balls in my stomach. It feels thick and solid, like I've eaten a huge meal of terror. It pushes upward, clogging my chest, blocking my throat, filling my mouth. I almost run for the bathroom, since I'm sure I'm about to throw up. Instead, when I open my mouth, words come out.

My voice, thin and quavery, fills the room. Syllables, sentences, then whole sections of my piece spill out. I'm talking. Too fast. The words, once started, won't stop until I reach the end. When I sit down, I count the minutes on my fingers and realize I've only used six of the eight.

I don't recover until after the third student reads. During the fourth and fifth speakers, I lean forward slightly and listen hard. Tory has instructed us to do "mini-critiques" on all the other competitors and to take notes in our speech team binder. We need to examine their strengths and weaknesses and use that knowledge to improve our own performance.

My heart sinks, filling up the spot left empty from the fear. The heat starts as a pinprick in my cheeks, but the flush spreads across my face. My fingertips feel like ice against my skin. While I can barely remember my performance, I didn't think it was that awful.

Until now. These kids could be on television or up on stage. The last kid has a voice so deep, he almost sounds like the narrator for the Harry Potter audio books. And since this kid is reading *Oliver Twist*, he even has the English accent perfected.

When the round is over and we all file out of the room, I know the truth. No one will look me in the eye. The single glance thrown my way is filled with pity. I was right. This is just like a reality TV show, and I'm the one clueless contestant who doesn't know how terrible she is. Except. I do know.

I duck my head and rush for the drinking fountain. I take long swallows of water, letting it chill me and fill my stomach. I hope it will wash away the fear.

It doesn't. If my second round isn't worse, then it isn't any better either. I hang on, telling myself that I'm more than halfway done with the day. One more round to go. In my third and final classroom, I sink gratefully into a desk near the center of the room.

A new set of kids filters in, one of them a boy with summer green eyes. Those eyes light up when he sees me. He holds up a finger, telling me to hang on for just a second, then heads for the judge at the back of the room. They speak so quietly, I can't catch their words. Of course, the blood is roaring so loudly in my ears, they could be shouting and I still couldn't hear them.

Sam plops down in a desk next to mine. "Hey," he says. "I'm double entered, so I had to tell her—" He nods at the judge. "That I need to speak first." He grins at me. "So. Looks like you took my advice."

I nod.

"Prose," he continues. "Good choice. Are you also doing story-telling?"

For a moment, I can only stare. Why would he think that? "N-no," I stammer. "Just this."

"For the first year, that's probably best. I tried a bunch of categories last year, and it was kind of crazy. Fun, but crazy."

"We'll start in a minute," the judge calls out.

Sam widens his eyes in mock terror. "I'll see you in the final round if not before. Okay?"

I don't have words to answer. Does he think I'll be in the final round—or just watching it? Before I can sort this out, the judge speaks again.

"First up, W-3, Sam Romero."

He stands up and heads for the front of the room.

Sam Romero? Really? As in Sam *Romeo* Romero? Winnetka's star speaker *is* my Sam from the park. The breath is stuck in my throat. In fact, I'm pretty sure I've forgotten how to breathe. I'm so wrapped up in this, and Sam, and Romeo, that I almost miss the title of the piece he's reading. Almost.

Flowers for Algernon.

It's the third time I've heard it today, but the first that it blows me away. I'm in tiny pieces, close to crying, when Sam finishes reading.

"Like it?" Sam asks when he's back at his desk.

With my palm, I push the start of a tear from my eye. I manage a nod.

"Great." He gathers his things. "Gotta run, but I'll see you around."

Now, I'm floating. *See ya around.* What does that mean—exactly? My head is so full of Sam's words that I don't hear the judge speak, or at least, don't hear what she says until a note of irritation pierces the soft cloud of my thoughts.

"F-13, are you ready?"

Oh, I am so not ready. I grab my script and walk to the front of the room. It's a terrible reading, but that doesn't matter because of two things:

1. It's the last round for the day.
2. Sam isn't here to see it.

And that's all I need to make it through the next eight minutes.

———

IN THE AUDITORIUM, I sit with Savannah, Kaitlin, and the rest of the Fremont team. Kids from Winnetka crowd three full rows dead center, right in front of the stage. We are puny and unworthy by comparison.

Tory pushes her way down our row. When she reaches the seat next to mine, she makes Kaitlin get up and move.

"Okay," she says to me, "we need the scoop."

I have no idea what she's talking about.

"Details. What piece is he doing for prose?" Tory continues, then raises her voice. "We have nothing on his piece for humorous interpretation since *someone* forgot to sit in on the humorous interp final round."

"Because *someone* had two final rounds of his own." Ryan's voice comes from the row behind us. "Yeah. That's right. *Two*."

I glance over my shoulder. He looks smug. Tory tosses her head, choosing to ignore the remark. Their bickering makes me miss my brother Derek.

"Anyway, we need to know what's up with him." Tory points toward the Winnetka team.

I play dumb. I squint, turn my head slightly as if I'm searching the crowd. I pretend I don't see the boy standing in the center of the Winnetka team, fist bumping and high fiving.

"Give me what you got on him," Tory says.

"Who?" I'm good at this dumb thing. I even sound that way to myself.

She jerks an arm toward Winnetka. At that moment, Sam glances over. From this distance, I can't see the light in his green eyes, but we all see him wave.

"Did Sam Romero just *wave* at you?" Tory asks.

Did he? I'm not one hundred percent sure. "Maybe he was waving at you."

Behind me, Ryan cracks up. Ben has to pound him on the back before he can settle down.

"You watched the finals, right?" Tory is back to business.

I nod. "He was in my third round, too."

"What piece is he doing?"

A smile tugs at the corners of my mouth. I don't answer right away, even though the anticipation is killing Tory. At last, I take pity. *"Flowers for Algernon."*

"Oh, you've got to be kidding me."

"Nope."

Tory swivels in her seat. "Ry!" she calls out. When he looks her way, she mouths, "He's doing *Algernon.*"

Ryan makes his face go all bug-eyed in shock. "No way."

Tory points at me. "Eyewitness."

"They're messing with us," he says. "It's the only explanation."

Tory turns back around and leans her head toward mine. Her voice drops, so only I can hear what she's saying. "They did this last year. Their coach had Romero *all* over the place until the Big 9 tournament, the one right before sub-sectionals. Then he killed in prose."

Before she can tell me more, the Worthington speech team coach comes out on stage to present the awards. Twice, Tory scoots past me to accept first place in extemporaneous speaking and a ribbon in discussion. Ryan flip flops with a ribbon in informational speaking and second place in discussion.

Now Tory looks smug and Ryan seems fascinated by the ceiling. When the Worthington coach announces the first place winner for humorous interpretation, the name Sam Romero echoes throughout the auditorium. The Winnetka team goes wild. On his way up the stage stairs, Sam trips. My heart catches. I almost cry out. Then he rolls and springs to his feet, the whole thing an act worthy of a Shakespeare play.

The Winnetka team cheers even louder. A few whistles cut through the noise, and a chant of, "Ro-me-o, Ro-me-o, Ro-me-o," sweeps over the audience. Tory taps my shoulder. I freeze, my lips in mid-chant, and peer at her. She rolls her eyes.

"This is why we need info on Romero," she says as the crowd settles. "I don't believe for a second that their coach is positioning him for state with *Algernon*." She makes a gagging noise. "Something's up."

When Sam takes first in prose, it's a repeat performance, except without the fall. He strides across the stage every inch the serious speaker, and the girls in my row start chanting. They don't stop, not even when Tory glares at them. But I do, if for no other reason than Sam Romeo Romero did not hear me speak during the third round. I clutch the megaphone charm Caro gave me and send a long, shuddering *thank you* skyward.

Chapter 5

ONE DOWN, *eight to go* is my mantra all week long. I chant it so often in my head that once, when Tory's camera is trained on me, it pops out of my mouth.

"What?" she says and switches off the recording.

"She's killing off all the team members," Ryan says. "She started with Ben."

Who is actually at wrestling practice.

"And I thank her," Ryan continues as if I'm not even in the room. "As long as she leaves me a few of the P&P girls."

This is what he calls all the girls doing prose or poetry—and really, that's just me, Savannah, and Kaitlin. Which of the two does he like? They both like him. They're also best friends. This could get messy, in a reality TV show kind of way.

I practice all week, but I don't put much heart—or worry—into it. I'm convinced the next tournament will be a breeze, not that I'll win a prize or even score above a five. But the worst is over. I know what to expect. I know failure can't actually kill me.

And that Saturday, I do breeze through the first two rounds. I ignore my own performance and concentrate on filling out notes and critiques on the other contestants. This is actually a requirement for lettering in speech team, which I don't care about. However, even though Mr. Henderson hasn't said anything, I suspect it's a requirement for passing speech class.

We're two speakers into the third round. The judge is scratching a few words on her critique sheets before calling the next speaker. I'm bracing for that to be me when the door to the classroom eases open.

It's Sam.

"Sorry," he says, his voice quiet and apologetic. "I'm double entered, in this and great speeches—"

The judge waves him in. "Take a seat and catch your breath. We'll start in a moment with—" She thumbs through her sheets. "F-13, Jolia Cuppernull."

I can't force myself to look at Sam. I run my finger along the edge of my piece, the words blurring until all I see is forest green—oak leaf green. Why didn't I think of this? Why did I think it would be easy? I'd rather take Jane's place on that stool and stand for a hundred hours than speak in front of Sam.

But I don't have a choice. My limbs feel stiff, like they're carved from oak. I grip my script until I tear a bit of the construction paper. I can't remember any of the words I speak, but I do know this: they come out all wrong.

———

WHY IS it worse to fail in front of someone you know?

The lobby is quiet, and certainly the trophies in their cases are not going to answer me. From down the hallway comes chatter from the cafeteria. That's where most everyone is, trading horror stories from their rounds, congratulating Tory and Ryan for making the finals—again. Some of the voices carry an excitement so tense,

I think their owners might shatter. Other voices are almost sleepy with relief.

What would everyone hear in my voice? What does humiliation sound like? I know I should go to the cafeteria, read the judges' critiques of my performance, eat lunch—but I don't have the stomach for any of that.

The soft squeak of sneakers alerts me to someone coming down the hall. Tory clip clops in heels. Ryan clomps no matter what's on his feet. Mr. Henderson walks like a teacher, and there's no mistaking that.

This is someone else.

In the trophies' reflection, I see a fringe of dark bangs. If I turn, I know his eyes will look like summer. In the glint from the trophies, they look golden. But I don't turn around.

"Hey," Sam says, after a long moment.

"Hey," I say, not to him, but to his golden reflection.

"I like your piece," he says. "It fits you."

"Yours, too."

"Yeah, I know a lot of kids do it."

A lot? I heard something from *Flowers for Algernon* twice today. Tory was right. Except when it comes to Sam. Even the second time around, his performance made my throat clog up. I had to blink hard and fast to keep the tears away. For eight minutes, he made me forget what a disaster my own reading was.

"But it's my favorite," he says. "I've probably read it twelve times."

I turn around since this is about books. I love books. From what I remember, Sam does too. I almost bring up the park, but that seems so long ago and so silly. Instead, I say, "I think I've only read *Jane Eyre* four or five times."

"It's really long, so that probably makes us even."

For the first time today, I laugh. He grins back.

"So what do you think of speech tournaments?" he says.

"It's like a reality TV show without the cameras."

He stares for a moment, then coughs out a laugh. "Yeah. I guess so. Kind of like a literary American Idol."

"They could call it So You Think You Can Talk."

"Or Speech Survivor," Sam says. "You have to make the finals to stay on the island."

"Good thing for me it isn't."

Our conversation crashes to a halt. I want to shut my eyes or turn away, but I can't. I want to take back my stupid words, but I can't do that either.

Out of desperation, I say, "Did you make the finals?" I know the answer, since I saw *Romero, Sam* on the finalist list for both serious prose and great speeches.

A hint of pink spreads across his cheeks. "Yeah."

"I'll be there," I say. It's one of the team rules. If you don't make the final round, you sit in on the one for your category. I can also add more notes to my speech binder, although I'm beginning to wonder if I'm not any good at speech how I'll ever pass. There are only so many notes I can take.

He gestures at the trophies, then drops his hand. He tugs on his tie, which is blue with a thin red stripe, and doesn't look like it belongs to his dad at all. At last, he says, "Would you like to be there?"

I blink and my mind goes blank. I'm certain I just told him I would. "I will be."

"No, would you like to be *there*."

He's asking something I'm not sure I can answer. "Do you ... I mean—"

"Would you like to be *in* the final round, not watching it?"

I shake my head, but I don't think I'm telling him no. I'm telling him that some things are impossible, and this is one of them.

"I could coach you," he says.

"You?" Not that I think Sam would make a bad coach. But he is clearly a Winnetka star speaker—just like Tory and Ryan said. Everywhere I went today, all I heard was gossip about Sam. "You know we're on different teams," I say, trying to make a joke of it. "Right?"

"So there's that rivalry thing." He shrugs. "We'll just have to keep it secret. It's like the Montagues and Capulets, only with scripts instead of swords."

Shakespeare. *Romeo and Juliet.* We read the play last year in Honors English. My thoughts go immediately to Romeo Romero, and my face burns. The pink returns to Sam's cheeks, and I wonder if he knows what all the girls say about him.

"At least think about it," he says.

I nod.

We leave the lobby together. When Sam and I walk down the crowded hallway to Room 33, a trail of whispers follows us. Only after Sam speaks and slips out of the room for the great speeches final, do I remember that *Romeo and Juliet* didn't have a happy ending.

———

SAM CATCHES me before I slip into the auditorium for the awards ceremony.

"Hey," he says, out of breath. He tugs me around a corner and pulls out his cell phone. "Do you have a cell?" he asks.

I nod.

"Do you have it now?"

I pull it from my skirt pocket.

"Can you receive texts?"

I nod again, wondering where this is going.

"Great. I have an idea for coaching. Next tournament, I'll find an empty room and then text you the number. Sound good?"

I try to speak, but my teeth get in the way.

"I mean, if you want to, that is." His words are rushed, but clear, and I wonder how he does that, how he makes his words do what he wants them to do.

"Just tell everyone you're going somewhere quiet to practice," he says. "No one will think anything of it."

Except that all the practice in the world can't help me. "What about you? Don't you need to practice before the first round?"

He shrugs like it's no big deal. Besides, I know the answer. I saw it today during the third and the final rounds. He doesn't need to practice.

"So. Phone number?"

I hold up my phone, number displayed, so he can punch it into his own phone. A moment later, my phone buzzes in my hand and a strange number pops up—Sam's number.

"Anytime next week," he says. "Just text me. Yes. Or no. But I hope it's yes." Then he heads into the auditorium, leaving me to stare at the screen of my phone.

———

BY THE TIME I make it to our row, everyone else is already there. Tory shoots me a glare, which I ignore. I slip in next to Kaitlin.

"So, the deal." Tory leans her head between ours. "Is he still doing *Algernon?*"

"He'll probably win with it, too," I say. "He killed in the final round."

"Gawd." Tory slumps in her seat. "I can't believe he's kicking our ass with *Flowers for Algernon.*"

When she recovers and starts talking with Ryan, Kaitlin whispers in my ear.

"You know why Tory has it in for Sam, right?"

I shake my head.

"Last year, she did prose along with extemporaneous speaking, you know." Kaitlin pauses. *"Flowers for Algernon."*

My mouth drops open.

"I swear it's true." She leans closer and lowers her voice even more. "And Tory used to follow Sam around. I think maybe." Kaitlin makes a face and squints at Tory. "Maybe she had a crush. I don't know. That's just what some of the Winnetka girls said." Kaitlin rolls her eyes like trusting anything the Winnetka girls say is the dumbest thing anyone could do. "Then guess what happened."

I can't guess at all, but I'm dying to know.

"At sub-sectionals, Sam did a scene from *Algernon*. Totally out of the blue," Kaitlin says. "He came in third and went to regionals."

"And Tory?"

"Fourth place. She's convinced Sam stole her slot and has hated him ever since."

Stole her slot—and her heart? I ease around and peer at Tory. She gives me that debater's stare, like she knows Sam Romero's number is on my cell phone. I spin back around and pretend to watch the rest of the awards.

I'm pretty sure reality TV shows are a lot less complicated.

———

"NOT ACCEPTABLE," Tory says to us later, after we've all been herded onto the school bus that will take us back to Fremont. "No fraternizing with the enemy."

"Huh?" Kaitlin says, glancing up from her phone.

Tory leans over the back of her seat and covers the cell phone with her hand. "That means no talking, no texting, nothing with the Winnetka team." She fries Kaitlin with a look until she cowers in her seat. I can't imagine what sin she's committed, but I suspect it has something to do with all the gossip she suddenly has.

"Well, Jolia was talking to Sam Romero," Savannah says.

I spin around, shocked she'd rat me out like this. But she's Kaitlin's best friend. I'd rat her out to save Caro, that's for sure.

"Before the awards. They were talking," Savannah continues. "Looked pretty cozy to me."

Okay. I wouldn't be that much of a rat. I think.

"Lucky," Kaitlin breathes.

Tory narrows her eyes at me. "Really?"

"We were talking about the third round." The whole bus can hear it for the lie it is. But what else can I say?

Tory's gaze sweeps over me. She's in award-winning debater mode, and it's like she's sizing up the competition, like she just now realizes I'm more than her spy in the prose category. Before she can say anything else, the bus rumbles beneath us, and the doors whoosh close.

"Just remember, Cuppernull." Tory plops down sideways in her seat so she can skewer me with one last look. "They call him Romeo for a reason."

Chapter 6

MONDAY AT LUNCH, Caro is late. I have my tray already. The healthy-for-you pizza looks almost edible, and it certainly smells that way. But with Caro's chair empty, I can't seem to find my appetite. Jeremy stares at the spot, a glum expression on his face. It's like lunch without Caro is torment because he might have to talk to me.

I feel the same way about him.

"Know where she is?" he says after the second bell rings.

"I saw her this morning."

I pull out my phone (we're not supposed to have them out during school hours). With the table shielding my hands, I check for any missed text messages. I'm still checking, thinking that somehow, staring will make a message magically appear, when someone taps my shoulder.

I jolt straight up and turn. Caro's mom, Mrs. Sulvana, stands right behind me. Jeremy looks like he can't swallow and spins away, scooting behind a few friends. Mrs. Sulvana doesn't notice. All her attention is on me.

"Jolia! I am here for PIE!" She says this loudly, too, although PIE—Parent Information Exchange—isn't something you eat but a meeting between parents and the school administration. It's also Mrs. Sulvana's version of a joke. And really, as far as parent jokes go, it's kind of funny, so I laugh.

"Have you seen Caro?" Mrs. Sulvana asks.

I shake my head. "Not since this morning."

"When you do, see if you can help her with the math." She sighs. "It was hard going last night."

"I will," I promise.

I'm tracking Caro's mom as she threads through the tables and chairs to the main doors. Kids grow quiet as she passes their tables. Even the jocks at Jeremy's table seem subdued for once.

Something slaps the back of my chair, and I jerk upright again, my heart pounding so hard, it aches. Peering over the top edge of a huge artist's portfolio is Caro. She grins at me, then hands me the huge leather folder.

"Your mom—" I begin.

"I know, I know." She rolls her eyes. "I was hiding until the start time for the PIE meeting. I wish she had a normal job like your mom."

Mrs. Sulvana runs her own specialty catering business—all Middle Eastern baked goods and desserts. Pastries and breads and everything that melts in your mouth. I love staying over at Caro's house. But her mom sets her own hours, which gives her plenty of time for volunteering.

Jeremy emerges from the jock table and mutters, "Hey, babe," before sitting back and talking with his friends, like now that Caro is actually here, he doesn't need or want to talk to her. I try not to roll my eyes, but can't help it. He is such a tool sometimes. Luckily, Caro doesn't see. She's too busy clearing the trays and blowing crumbs from the table.

"Look!" She flips open the portfolio.

The images on the paper take my breath away. Caro is going to be a famous artist someday, and here's the proof.

"What do you think?" she asks. "I was going insane on Saturday while you were at the tournament, so I started in on the first four panels—not that we have to use these," she says, her voice worried and edgy.

Every Saturday, Caro is trapped inside her house, babysitting her little sisters. Usually she calls, or we text, and we invent all sorts of things to keep her sisters from driving her up the wall. But of course, now my Saturdays are filled with speech tournaments. If this is the result, I should probably keep going.

"I had to do something," she adds. "It's mostly doodles."

It's mostly *not*. I stare at the first four panels for our graphic novel, our retelling of *Romeo and Juliet*. Even if Caro's version of Romeo looks so much like Jeremy, they could be twins, I love it. She's left all the speech bubbles and spots for sound effects and narrative blank, waiting for my words. I can't wait to write them.

Jeremy glances over. His nose wrinkles—just slightly—but I don't think Caro notices. Good thing, too—for him, at least. He just doesn't get this side of Caro. All year long, he's been trying to get her to drop creative storytelling. One day at lunch, he even said, "Graphic novels are for nerds."

Caro swung her hair around, pushed back her tray, and stalked from the cafeteria. I wanted to leap to my feet and give her a standing ovation. I wanted to tell Jeremy that he blew it—big time. Instead, I ran after her.

The next day, Jeremy brought in a bouquet of flowers (the kind you can get at the grocery store). All the girls squealed. Caro went pink. When Jeremy went down on one knee and apologized, all was forgiven. So many girls crowded around Caro, I could barely see her or the flowers. Jeremy's friends gave him a hard time, which is such a boy thing to do. But I'm sure most of them were just jealous.

Now I can't take my eyes off the start of our graphic novel. "This is better than anything you could buy at Comic World," I tell Caro—and I mean it.

Caro glows. "I can't wait until next term. Do you think we can get it published?"

Every year, Mrs. Riley selects a handful of the best projects and has them published through the school district's "Fremont Free Press" program. The year Derek took creative storytelling, he made a Claymation movie they featured on the school district website for months. Caro's artwork is certainly good enough. Now if I can just make the words match.

"Maybe," I say. Worry pings around inside me. Never mind making the words match, I have to make it to the next term and creative storytelling. There won't be a next term if I can't do something about this one.

So, sure, a modern retelling of *Romeo and Juliet* isn't my life. But the storytelling part? That is. It's one thing to talk about dreams; it's another to see them in black and white. It's like there's a mix of excitement and anxiety brewing inside me at the thought of doing this. But if I don't pass speech, I won't even get to try. Worse, Caro won't get to try either.

My gaze drifts toward the table where Tory and Ryan sit. I stare hard before looking at Caro's drawings again. She fusses with them, tucking them away before Jeremy or one of his friends can splatter ketchup all over them. I don't say anything. I simply slip my phone into my palm, hiding it from everyone, including Caro. The chair legs squeak when I push from the table. Quickly, before Caro can say anything, I rush from the cafeteria.

In the girls' bathroom, my heart thuds so hard it hurts. I slip into the last stall and lean against the door. My palms are sweaty and I have a hard time scrolling through the numbers on my phone. At last, that strange, new number pops up, and I type a single word.

Yes.

I wait so long to press send that the screen dims. Then I do press send, and I'm glad I never ate lunch. I might throw up. I might collapse right here because my legs feel like noodles. I can't believe I just told Sam yes.

But I realize there's no way I can tell him no.

―――――――

ALL WEEK LONG, I'm a bundle of nerves. I can't wait for Saturday. I dread Saturday. At lunch on Friday, I dip my French fries into apple sauce—then eat them anyway. This earns me a "Hard core!" and high five from Jeremy, and a disgusted head shake from Caro. She has sisters, so naturally, nothing all that gross ever happens at her house. If there's an upside to Jeremy, it's that she's learning what boys are *really* like.

At speech team practice, I botch my time in front of Tory's digital camera so badly, she shuts it off halfway through my piece.

"What's going on?" she says, her voice and eyes hard.

"What?" I don't know what I've done wrong, but from the look on Tory's face, it must be something.

"This isn't a joke, you know."

"What isn't?" I ask.

"Speech team. It's not a joke. Not to me, not to Ryan, not to the rest of the kids here."

"It's not to me, either." My words sound flat. It's my grade, I want to add. It's creative storytelling with Caro. It's the honors program and my diploma. Speech team is the furthest thing from a joke that I can think of. But maybe the joke is on the speech team —and I'm the punch line. In that case, I agree. It isn't funny at all.

"Right." Tory doesn't sound convinced. "You're done for today."

She turns to walk away and I reach out a hand to stop her,

thinking I will tell her everything, from the rink rats to failing speech to Sam. If she can help me, maybe Sam won't have to.

But she doesn't see me. Or more likely, she pretends not to. In the contest between not failing and going behind Tory's back, I know which one wins. So I don't say another word.

————

THAT NIGHT BEFORE THE TOURNAMENT, I make sure to plug in my cell phone so it will have a full charge. I pair my best black pleated skirt with a new blouse and knitted scarf I plan to loop around my neck. I search out deodorant and see my only choice is the vanilla chai. Smelling like a Starbucks is better than smelling, I decide.

I think I will be awake all night, but I fall asleep. In my dream, I've traded in my donkey teeth for a pair of rabbit ones. I look like Bugs Bunny, but I'm not nearly as funny.

The next morning, the bus bumps down the highway for sixty miles of nerve-jangling, bone-jarring anxiety. The ride is too long. Then, once we arrive, something inside me insists that it's been much too short. I'm not ready to face another three rounds.

I'm not ready to face Sam.

Like the last tournament, we group around a table in the cafeteria. The hum of chatter, stray lines from speeches, a few political arguments surround us—the air vibrates with them. So much so, I nearly miss my cell phone buzz. On it is a message from that strange, new phone number:

Sam: 33

That's it. I stand and shake out my skirt. I glance around as if searching for the bathrooms. I slip my script from beneath my mittens, then shove those into the pocket of my winter coat. I already have my room assignments for all three rounds, so I don't need to worry about that. I walk as if my only destination is the bathroom or a quiet place to practice.

Room 33 is on the second floor. The hallway is hushed, but muted voices come from behind a few closed doors. I hear a rattle of paper, a declaration of some kind. I wonder if it feels strange to speak to a completely empty room. My ballet flats tap against the floor and it's a long walk to room 33.

I think to myself: *Romeo, Romeo, wherefore art thou, Romeo?* Of course, I know Juliet isn't asking where he is. Still. I have to hold in a nervous burst of giggles.

At last I find the room. Sam is sitting in back, just like a judge would. He nods at me when I enter. Before I can say anything, he speaks up.

"Why don't we start the round? First up is entrant F-13."

Oh, I think. He is a judge, or pretending to be one, and I should play along. I clear my throat, head for the center of the room, and, after one shaky breath, begin my introduction to *Jane Eyre.*

"Okay, wait, stop, cut ... whatever." Sam stands, his Chuck Taylor All Stars slapping the linoleum. It's the only thing not proper about his outfit: perfect dress pants, a white shirt, the blue tie with the thin red stripe, and the bright red All Stars. Mr. Henderson wouldn't let him get away with that. Both Ryan and Ben clomp around in dress shoes. But I think it helps set Sam apart.

I'm only on the second page, but I pause and peer over the top of my script at him. He marches forward, stops directly in front of me, then pushes the top of my script lower, then lower still.

"Judges will mark you down if they can't see your face," he says. "Your script is not a prop, but it isn't a crutch, either. Or a shield. Okay?"

I nod.

"Let's start from the beginning," he says, heading back to his chair.

I'm maybe ten seconds in when he springs up and again heads straight for me. I take a step back.

"You're hiding," he says.

I shake my head, but the accusation makes me want to hide.

"No, you are." He shakes his own head like he's trying to shake out the solution to a problem. "I thought it was where I was sitting at last week's tournament, but as you speak, your script inches up until no one can really see you. I guarantee the judges will score you higher if they can see your face and believe you want to be here."

Well, that's the problem, isn't it? I *don't* want to be here. Tory knows it. The judges know it. And the way Sam is looking at me now?

He knows it too.

"The thing is—" He breaks off, tugs at his bangs in frustration. "I don't understand. You used to be so..."

"What?" The single word is more air than question. What? I used to be so ... *what?*

Sam stares like he's waiting for an answer. I don't know what—or who—I used to be during those summers we played in the park. I don't know what—or who—I am now. All I know is the hot sting of a single tear against my cheek and the feel of words trapped behind my teeth.

I run as fast as I can for the girls' bathroom.

———

I SPLASH my face and gulp water straight from the tap. Only then do I head for the bathroom's mirrors. I check my teeth with both my index finger and my tongue. They haven't moved, haven't changed size, haven't become the strangely grotesque donkey teeth I can still feel.

A flash of something blue with a red stripe appears in the

mirror's reflection. When a white dress shirt comes into view, my heart leaps. Sam. In the girls' bathroom. How long has he been standing there?

From his frown, I guess: long enough. I don't turn around.

"What are you doing?" he asks.

I've never seen myself blush before. The studious part of my brain—the small sliver of it that's still working, anyway—is kind of fascinated. The rest of me? Mortified. Sam. In the girls' bathroom. Watching me inspect my teeth.

Failing speech could never be worse than this.

"You shouldn't ..." he trails off like he's unsure what to say. I don't blame him. What do you say to the crazy girl obsessed with her teeth?

"I mean, it's just that you're so pretty. All the guys ... well, you're pretty, is all."

I shut my eyes, lean my forehead against the mirror, the glass cooling my skin. I don't move until I hear Sam's footfalls echo down the hall and fade away.

———

I'M ON MY BED, staring at the ceiling when my cell phone goes off, playing the ringtone that tells me it's Caro. I reach for the nightstand and miss. I reach again, grab the phone, and heave a sigh all at once.

Caro doesn't hear, or she's too excited, because all that comes through the speaker is: "Grand Slam! Grand Slam! Grand Slam!"

I know what this means. The thought of it makes me tired. Grand Slam and all the noise: the arcade, batting cages, mini-golf, and of course, laser tag. My arms and legs feel weighed down. I'm not sure how I'll get up to eat dinner, never mind spend three hours chasing after golf balls and shooting lasers under black lights.

"Everyone is going to be there." Caro says. This is code. Everyone = Jeremy and Jeremy's friends. Maybe Caro isn't allowed to date, but if she happens to be in the same place Jeremy is? Well, that would look like an accident. I know it's not. She works over-time arranging this sort of thing. I go along for the ride—and as their cover. I'm the perfect third wheel.

"I don't know," I say.

"You okay?" The excitement in her voice fades, replaced by concern. "You sound like someone beat you up."

I feel like someone has. Not that I have any bruises—not ones you can see anyway. The three rounds at today's tournament did nothing to erase the memory of Sam in the girls' bathroom. My scores were the lowest on the team—all fives. Everyone else improved.

I got worse.

To avoid Sam, I sat in on the finals for extemporaneous speak-ing. Tory took first—of course. But when she wasn't speaking, she was glaring at me. By the time I made it to the bus, I felt battle scarred.

"It was a rough day," I say to Caro. "I don't know if I'm ... earning enough extra credit with these tournaments." I hold my breath, hoping she can hear the truth inside my lies.

"I just don't get why you're doing it," she says instead.

I sink lower into the comforter on my bed. My pleated skirt, white blouse, and scarf are on the floor. I'm wearing my favorite pajama bottoms and a Doctor Who T-shirt. I have no plans to move until tomorrow.

"But maybe getting out and doing something fun would be good for you," Caro says.

"I bet you know just the place." I can't help it. I laugh.

"It's called Grand Slam. Ever hear of it?"

"I hear a bunch of cute guys go there," I say.

"Maybe we'll find one for you."

This time, my laugh sounds almost bitter. I'm happy for Caro, really. I don't need a boyfriend—at least, not one like Jeremy. But I wish we didn't plan everything we do around him.

"Will you go?" she asks, a plaintive note in her voice.

"You have to feed me," I say. Caro has a ton of money from babysitting her little sisters, so this is no problem.

"Done and done. We'll be by at seven thirty."

My phone goes silent. I scroll through my recent text messages. The last one is Sam's, inviting me to room 33. My finger hovers over the button to reply. But what would I say? Sorry for being a freak?

I turn off my phone before I can add to the day's humiliation.

CARO'S MOM pulls their Honda into the parking lot of Grand Slam and stops at the front door. She turns around to inspect the two of us sitting in the backseat.

"You girls sure love this place," she says.

Well, Jeremy loves it, which is why we always end up here.

"Where else are we going to play mini-golf in the winter?" Caro says. It's a question that doesn't need an answer. Because honestly? Caro sucks at mini-golf.

"I'll be back at eleven thirty," Caro's mom says. Her lilting accent makes her sound gentle, but she points a fierce finger at the front door. "Right here."

I thank her as I climb down from the minivan. The sky is clear above us, but the glare from the big red letters on top of the building hides all the stars. I tilt my head back, hoping to see one or two anyway.

I don't.

Inside, noise explodes around us. At eight p.m., the price for a wristband drops, and you can get unlimited mini-golf, batting cages, and laser tag for half price. Already, boys from the baseball team line the cages, the thwack of the aluminum bats and rattle of chain link in the air.

We stand in line, and Caro squints while she scans the crowd, looking for close-cropped black curls and a swaggering jock walk. Jeremy finds us first. He spins Caro around and she squeals.

"Happy late Valentine's Day." Jeremy pulls an envelope from his back pocket. Caro tears it open and out spills a gold necklace with a heart pendant. She squeals again, throws her arms around his neck, and gives him a big kiss. The nauseating truth hits me then. The three of us are on a Valentine's Day date.

This is so wrong.

"I can't believe you got out of prison," he says to her.

Caro points at me. "Thank Jolia."

Jeremy nods and I do the same. I want to ask where *my* present is, but for Caro's sake, I don't. If not for her, Jeremy and I probably wouldn't know each other's names. We don't fight, not exactly. Sometimes we'll take passive-aggressive swipes at each other. Hey, I have a brother. I know where all the weak spots are. But we're not friends and never will be.

"I'm holding a place in line for laser tag," he says. "Go there first."

So we do, with bright yellow bands circling our wrists and coins for the batting cages (which we'll give to Jeremy) in our pockets. People behind us grumble as we budge in line next to him.

He leans around us and says, loudly, "They had to buy their wristbands."

Like somehow that explains everything.

Laser tag is my favorite thing at Grand Slam. I'm pretty good at it, too. This is one of the advantages of having an older brother. You have to be quick and tricky if you ever want to win. Laser tag is also one of the few times Jeremy and I get along. We always form a team. Jeremy likes to make a big deal out of "protecting" Caro, but you don't get any points that way.

Besides, at least once per game, she ends up shooting one, if not both, of us in the back. Her laser tag skills are second only to her mini-golf ones.

Lasers flash, the black light makes my shoelaces glow a ghostly purple. There's a bunch of jocks from Winnetka opposite us. Jeremy signals for me to go one way while he creeps around the other. I sidestep a few middle school kids who have no clue what they're doing. I catch sight of Jeremy again.

At the same moment, we spring, laser guns firing.

Lights flicker. The sensors on the boys' vests blink on and off, a sure sign of a direct hit. Everyone scrambles. I lose sight of Jeremy. In front of me, a wall of Winnetka boys blocks my way. I dance around the one whose laser still works, getting off a shot to disable him. Then I slip right through.

No matter how many times we play, no matter how many times they see me here, they never expect a girl to take them out. I rush toward the corner we use as home base, triumph wiping away the truly awful day. I love laser tag. Caro was right. I did need some fun.

Up ahead, Jeremy is guarding Caro, but he's jerking his head around, like he's looking for me. I bound forward just as someone else cuts across my path.

We collide, me and this boy. I stagger backward, my free hand flailing. I raise my laser gun to shoot, but shock freezes my finger on the trigger. The boy in front of me?

Sam.

He gapes at me, his own gun slack in his hand. His vest covers most of his T-shirt, but from what I can see, I think it's a Doctor Who one.

I think maybe we'll stand like this forever, the two of us staring at each other, never saying a word. Then the sensors on my vest flash. Caro jumps forward and stares at her gun like she can't believe it's gone off. She clamps a hand over her mouth, but I'm too busy staring at Sam to hear her apology.

———

THE LIGHTS GO UP, harsh fluorescent ones that make my eyes ache. The attendants herd us all out so the next group can have their ten minutes of laser heaven. I'm shoved through the door right behind Sam, my hands raised. If someone pushes just a little bit harder, I'll end up grabbing his shoulders.

I hold my breath until we're all the way out into the hallway. Then I sink against a wall, my eyes closed.

"I'm starving," Jeremy says.

Of course he is. There's never a time he's not hungry. Although, truthfully, up until I saw Sam, I'd been hoping for a large pepperoni pizza. I know this is what Jeremy wants. He doesn't disappoint.

"Pizza!" he calls out, like a battle cry. We all move, Jeremy, his friends, Caro and me—and Sam.

He still hasn't said a word to me, but then I haven't said anything either, not even hello. I cast him a wary look, trying to hide behind my hair. At the same moment, our gazes touch, and we both flinch as if we've been burned.

Once we're in line at the food counter, Jeremy turns and gives Sam a sock on the shoulder. "Yo," he says, "You running track this year?"

Jeremy knows Sam? I inch closer so Sam is in my field of vision. He knows Jeremy?

"Yeah, I'll be there," Sam says. "Not sure what I'm running yet. Sprints. Maybe a relay."

Jeremy nods. "What about a field event? Coach wants to get me into high jump."

They start talking about heights and times and splits. I glance at Caro and she rolls her eyes at me. Her look says it all: *Boys. What can you do?*

My mind whirls. So along with being a Winnetka star speaker, Sam is also a jock? This boy, who plays at being Romeo and wears Doctor Who T-shirts, also tears up the ground with his feet? At least, that's how Jeremy is making it sound. I wonder. Will Caro want to go to Jeremy's track meets this year?

I might decide to come along, at least when they run against Winnetka.

Once we get our pizza, Sam splits off from us. He sits with a group from Winnetka—I recognize a few boys from the speech tournament. After we eat, I'm swept away by Jeremy and Caro and all of Jeremy's friends. I don't see Sam. By the time eleven o'clock rolls around and we're playing one last round of mini-golf, I don't think I will.

I've searched—without trying to look like I'm searching—for him all night. I don't want to leave without seeing him again. What I'll say if I do see him, I don't know.

Caro hits a hole in one—for a hole we're not even playing—and Jeremy dashes off to retrieve her ball. My cell phone vibrates against my leg. I pull it from my pocket and see that same strange number again.

Sam's number.

Sam: I have an idea.

I glance from the screen and scan the area. Sam is standing across from me at the counter where you turn in all your arcade tickets for prizes. His thumbs fly across his phone's keyboard and a second later, my phone buzzes again.

Sam: you guys have Friday off?

Instead of replying, I glance up and meet those incredible green eyes. For a moment, I can't respond at all, but at last manage a single nod. Friday is a teacher workshop day, for all Minnesota schools.

But why doesn't he just walk across the lobby and talk to me? A few kids from the Winnetka speech team cut across the area on their way to laser tag. From the arcade, I see Tory and Ryan step out, fistfuls of tickets sprouting from their hands. They head straight for the prize counter, each bumping Sam's shoulder when they pass. Nice. I sigh. Keep it classy, guys. Keep it classy.

But I understand why. No fraternizing with the enemy. It works both ways. My phone buzzes for a third time.

Sam: We could get together. Unless you are mad at me.

I type back.

Jolia: Not mad.

I leave it at that, since I'm not sure what else to say. Is he still coaching me? After today's disaster, I find that hard to believe. But then, it's also hard to believe I'm standing thirty feet away from Sam Romero while he sends me text messages.

Sam: Fri. afternoon? Maybe library, but will send text.

Jolia: Ok

From across the lobby, Sam looks up from his phone. He smiles, a totally secret smile meant just for me. Even as my heart squeezes, I wonder if Tory is right, if there's something I should worry about. But right now, all I want to do is believe in the boy with the summer-green eyes, the fast feet, and a way with words.

Chapter 7

FREMONT, Minnesota is melting. All week long, the temperature inches upward until, on Friday afternoon, the weather widget on Dad's laptop says it's fifty degrees.

"The dog and I need a walk," Mom declares when she comes home from work early. She's a programmer for a software company. Dad is a freelance writer and has, for as long as I can remember, worked from home. Our dog Toby starts spinning in a circle the second Mom pulls the leash from its hook by the kitchen door.

"Enjoy it while you can," Dad says. "Winter isn't over yet."

Mom and Toby leave the house, her chant of "La, la, la, I can't hear you," echoing until the door closes. Dad laughs. He heads to the kitchen to brew some more coffee. I love the smell, but it tastes like charred mud unless I add a ton of cream and sugar. Mom says it's an acquired taste.

It feels strange to be home on a Friday. Ever since the clock hit 12:01, my legs have felt twitchy, and my fingers creep toward my cell phone. I've checked the display at least once every fifteen minutes.

"Plans this afternoon, Jo?" Dad asks. He takes the cream from the fridge and pours some into a mug. Apparently he's noticed my jittery state as well.

"Maybe," I say as my cell phone vibrates. My heart leaps into action, beating so fast I think it might fly out of my chest.

I pull out my phone, bracing for disappointment, certain it's only Caro sending a save-my-sanity message as she babysits her younger sisters. They are five, seven, and nine, and she should get hazard pay for what she goes through, especially on a day off from school.

But the message on my phone is from Sam.

Sam: Meet at the park?

As in Meadow Park? *Our* park? My fingers tremble. I can't hit the right letters and end up backspacing three different messages.

Sam: Too nice for indoors.

I agree. If only I could get my fingers to tell him that. My palms feel damp, my stomach hollow. My heart races with fear that I won't be able to answer him in time.

Sam: You there?

Jolia: Yyyes

That's it. It's like I've grown hooves to go along with my donkey teeth. At this rate, I won't be able to communicate at all.

Sam: Park in 10?

Jolia: Yes

Sam: see ya.

I nod at the phone, which might be the stupidest thing I've ever done. I glance up. Dad is sipping coffee and giving me an odd look, like maybe I really have sprouted donkey hooves and ears to match.

"Important message?" he asks.

"Sort of." Reality hits me then. Ten minutes. I glance down. Do I look okay? Should I change? I start for my room, then blurt, "Can I go to the park?"

"By yourself?" Dad frowns at his coffee. "Isn't Caro babysitting?"

"I'm meeting a friend from speech."

Technically, this is not a lie. Sam was my summer best friend, which could make him my friend now. And he's from a speech team—just not my speech team.

"Is your phone charged?"

I hold up my cell so Dad can see it.

"Good. Call if you need anything."

Meadow Park is only a quarter of a mile away. Derek and I spent a big chunk of our summers there, while Dad worked on his laptop in the shade of the gazebo. We learned all its patterns, like when the playground was too crowded with toddlers or too hot from the afternoon sun. Every summer, after Caro left for the Sulvana's endless cross-country trip to visit their huge extended family, I played.

At first, I was all alone. I created my own worlds and dramas. If no one else was around, Derek might play with me, but I was fine on my own. When a boy my own age started showing up at the same times we did, it felt like an intrusion. This boy had a way of budging in on my games and into my imagination. It was like he could see inside my head, knew where I'd built castles in the air, and wanted to move in.

I hid from him, but he was so persistent, it looked—and felt—like a game of hide and seek. Once, when I took refuge beneath some bushes near the gazebo, I had a rare moment of peace. Until I heard the boy's father talking to Dad.

"I hate to keep him cooped up in the house all summer. At least I can work from home, but the rest of it?" The boy's dad shook his head. "Ever since his mom left …"

The boy's dad continued to talk, but a buzzing in my head blocked all his words. I couldn't imagine my mom leaving, and my throat felt like some invisible hand had squeezed it hard. I crawled from the bushes, leaves caught in my shirt and hair, and went to find the boy.

He stood high in the jungle gym, hand shading his eyes, his gaze searching, searching, searching.

For me?

I climbed up, my breath coming in hard pants, my chest so tight, I thought my lungs might burst. When he saw me, he didn't smile. I inched across the walkway that circled the structure, careful to step over the seams where one section met the other—we never stepped on those. I wasn't sure what I was going to say, and when I finally reached him, I still had no idea.

At last, I simply said, "I'm Jolia."

"I'm Sam."

"Do you want to play?" I asked.

"I thought we already were."

Just like that, Sam and I were friends. And he knew my castles in the air by heart.

Now I navigate the streams of water that flow downhill toward the park. The sun warms my cheeks, but there's no hint of spring in the air. Everything smells cold and damp. Dad is right. Winter isn't over. But today, I'm pretending that it is. It's only when I reach the park—and see Sam sitting on a bench near the swings—that panic hits me.

I forgot my script. I look at my hands as if it will somehow magically appear there. My legs stutter to a stop. Before me, the park is a quilt of alternating patches of brownish-green grass and dirty snow. I'm about to pivot on my toes, rush all the way home, and grab *Jane Eyre*, when Sam waves.

My half-wave in return is pretty lame.

The sun heats my neck, dread fills my stomach, and the boy with the summer eyes fills my view. I open my mouth to apologize, to tell him I'll run home and get my script, but he speaks first.

"I thought we'd try something different today." Sam is holding two scripts and hands one to me.

Romeo and Juliet.

What does he want me to do with this? How can I get better at reading *Jane Eyre* by working on something else?

"This is a new way to practice," he says. "We're going to do the balcony scene."

I think over the plot of *Romeo and Juliet* and the balcony scene in particular. Is there a ... kiss in that scene? My mind blanks. In one of the movies? But is that a Hollywood thing or a Shakespeare thing? I flip through the pages, hoping Shakespeare will help me out, but his words are blurred and garbled, my fingers trembling, my heart hammering much too hard.

"Here." Sam takes my script and opens it to the correct page.

I peer at him and wonder if this is what Tory meant about Romeo Romero.

"Only," he says, "I'll be Juliet, and you'll play Romeo."

"What?" comes out with a squeak.

"Role reversal. It'll be fun."

"Fun?" Do we still kiss if he's Juliet and I'm Romeo? Maybe in this version of the play, Romeo tells Juliet that he's just not that into her. Except. I'm Romeo. And I can't help it. I'm very much into Sam.

"You don't look like Juliet," I say.

He laughs and rushes off to the edge of the woods. From there, he yanks handfuls of dead weeds and secures them to his head with his Twins baseball cap. He spins around and poses, one hand on his hip, the other behind his head.

I'm smiling so hard it hurts. Something warm and happy bubbles inside me, but it's mixed with a quick sting of tears. Who else would do something like this for me, except maybe Caro? I blink fast and clap until my palms sting all so Sam won't notice any dampness in my eyes.

Several tree branches lie at my feet, victims of this winter's ice storm. I find the driest and test it out. I brandish my sword and this time, Sam applauds.

"Ready?" he asks.

I whip my sword around, then nod.

"Let me get up to my balcony." He scales the jungle gym and edges along the upper walkway until he's near the climbing wall. "You can climb up there," he says, pointing to the wall with its red hand and footholds.

Climb up and then what? I think my mouth is hanging open. The air is cold against my lips and tongue, and I can taste dank mud and dead leaves.

Sam stares at me and I glance at the script. Yes, that's right. Romeo starts the scene, and I'm Romeo.

"But, soft! what light through yonder window breaks? It is the east, and ..." I hesitate, because I'm not really looking at a Juliet. "... and Romero is the sun."

Sam raises an eyebrow, and his lips twitch, like he's trying not to laugh. I continue. I don't remember Romeo saying so much, or things like: *O, it is my love!* and *O, that I were a glove upon that hand, That I might touch that cheek!*

I know it's probably impossible to get sunburn during February in Minnesota, but my face feels that hot. I'm certain the blush will never leave my cheeks.

Sam sighs Juliet's *Ay me!* and I speak a few more lines until it's his turn to say those famous ones:

"Jolia, Jolia, wherefore art thou, Jolia?" Sam pauses, looking pleased with the way my name sounds in the scene. "Deny thy father and refuse thy name, for if thou wilt not but be sworn my love, and I'll no longer be a Capulet."

I hear the echo of my next lines in my head: *Shall I hear more, or shall I speak at this?*

I *am* about to speak when a whoop cuts through the air. The sound is followed by the splash of bicycle tires slicing through water and the splatter of damp footsteps. I freeze, my fingertips crushing the script in my hand. My other hand goes slack, and I nearly drop the tree branch. The whoop comes again, the sound tearing through me. I know who it is without looking.

It's Crandall, Meadow Park's alpha rink rat—and he's brought along reinforcements.

Chapter 8

CRANDALL RIDES around the jungle gym, planting a foot at each turn and letting the wheels of his bike shoot mud with a force so strong, it covers everything. Mud hits the gazebo, the little kids' play area, the water fountain. Some hits my cheek. When I lick my lips, grit fills my mouth.

"Are we interrupting something?" Crandall skids to a stop near the climbing wall, near me.

"Go away," Sam says. His voice rings strong from up above, but his hands tug nervously at the weeds beneath his hat. He can't pull them out fast enough, and I can tell Crandall notices.

"It's a free country," Crandall says, "and a free park. And I want to ride my new bike." As he speaks, he points, sending a boy to each corner of the jungle gym. "Hey, bay-bee," he says to me, "what do you think of my new bike?"

I don't say anything. Crandall pops a wheelie and then spins around. It's a trick bike, and I'm guessing it was expensive. Derek thought about buying one but decided it wasn't worth the price.

I take a step forward, but Crandall brings the bike down, the front wheel nearly brushing my toes. I jump back.

His laugh sends a shiver through me. I don't know how we're going to get out of this. My phone is in my jeans pocket, but my hands are full of script and stick. With my eyes never leaving Crandall, I inch my hand toward my pocket. Maybe I can hide the phone behind the script. If I can just call Dad.

Crandall whips his bike in a tighter circle around me. I jerk my arms up to protect my face. The tree branch makes a hollow thunk against the bike's handlebars.

"Watch it!" he says and spins even closer. "My dad paid a lot for that."

Footsteps pound above my head. Up on the walkway, Sam hovers. The other three boys block the routes down the slides and climbing wall. He's trapped. I'm trapped. Still, he leans forward and shouts.

"Leave her alone!"

Crandall glances up and his lip curls. "You don't think he's—" He points at Sam. "Your *boyfriend*, do you? Why don't you want to go out with me, bay-bee?" Crandall's voice goes all smooth, like he's trying to be charming. This scares me even more. He gestures at Sam again. "You know *he* wants to."

From all sides, the boys laugh. Sam dashes up and down the walkway. He's trying to fake them out, I can tell, trying to find a way down to me. He ignores the insults and the laughter. He's not scared or frozen like I am, but he's not going anywhere either.

Crandall whips his bike around again, edging me away from the jungle gym. I know that's bad, *very* bad—in a way I can't let myself comprehend. No matter what happens, I can't leave Sam. I glance up and catch the worry in his green eyes. I think he mouths, "Can you run?"

But Crandall has me trapped like a scared rabbit. He rides so close, our jackets brush, and the smell of his sweat makes my stomach turn. I inch close to the jungle gym just as he swerves for me. I have nowhere to go. He isn't stopping.

His front tire runs over my foot.

I yelp, more from surprise than pain. Muddy tire tracks stain my green All Stars. Crandall pulls the bike around, ready for another pass. He's not afraid to hurt me, which means he's not afraid to hurt Sam either. From the corner of my eye, I see one of the other boys start to climb up a slide.

Crandall aims his bike straight at me. Tires churn the mud. I tighten my grip on the tree branch and brace my legs. Right before he reaches me, right before the treads connect with my feet, I ram the branch through the spokes of his front tire.

For an instant, the world stops. I see everything. The snapped branch. Crandall's mouth in a little O, his eyes wide with shock. The back of the bike tipping upward, like a bucking bronco.

Then the world speeds up again. Crandall flips over his handlebars. The bike goes careening, and he lands in a snowdrift. He doesn't move.

I've killed him, I think. *I've killed him.* Something grips my lungs. I can't take a full breath. I can't think. All I know is he tried to hurt us, and now I've killed him. What does that mean? A trial? Jail? Do they put you in jail for self-defense?

I barely hear the footfalls behind me. Someone grabs my hand. His grip is warm, my fingers like ice. "Come on," Sam whispers, his voice urgent.

He tugs, but my legs refuse to move. My mouth, too. I can't even explain to Sam that I've killed Crandall.

A groan fills the air. "Son of a—" comes from the snowdrift. Then, like some sort of Midwestern Yeti, Crandall bursts from the snow. "My bike! You little ... you broke my bike!"

Sam tugs harder. This time, my legs wake up. With our hands clasped, we run. We run as fast as we can. And Sam is the boy who can tear up the ground with his feet.

"I'm telling my dad!" Crandall shouts after us. "He'll sue you for everything you've got!"

We race across the street, leaving the park and the rink rats behind us. Sam leads me one way, then the next, through back-yards until we break away from the houses completely and into a field.

My legs churn. The ground is uneven and I stumble, my feet getting caught in ruts.

"Where … are we?" I pant more than ask.

"Nature preserve." He sounds just as breathless.

I halt, gazing around. I don't think I've been here before. For an instant I forget everything—the rink rats, Sam holding my hand, how cold and damp my feet are.

"Come on." Sam tugs my hand.

In the distance, I hear something that could be sneakers pounding wet asphalt. My shoes make a sucking sound when I pull them from the mud, and I run as fast as the earth will let me.

The nature preserve borders a playground for an apartment complex. I think we've run in a huge circle, but I don't ask. Sam pulls me inside an open garage and we hunker down behind a pickup truck.

For a long time, all we do is pant, breath echoing in our ears. I listen for other sounds, the ones that mean Crandall has followed us. A few birds chirp. A bell from a little girl's princess bike rings out.

I look around at the garage. It smells like oil and sawdust. There's a workbench to one side. The truck barely fits. We're squeezed in between its front and a canoe.

We're still holding hands.

"Where are we?" I ask.

"My house," Sam says. "Well, my garage." He hits the truck with his script. After everything, he still has it. I glance down and see that, in the hand not holding Sam's, I clutch my copy.

"I figured my house was closer, and if they were watching, they won't know where you live."

"Then." I swallow hard. My throat feels dry, my stomach like I might throw up. "What if he—I mean, do you think he's going to tell his dad? What if he sues?"

"Not going to happen." Sam sounds so sure about that. He must see the doubt on my face, because he keeps talking. "What is he going to say?" He drops his voice in an exact imitation of Crandall. "Hey, Dad, I was harassing this girl and she fought back, and now my bike is broken."

I laugh. His imitation is so spot-on, right down to his expression. Some of the fear inside me melts. Sam smiles, and I find it hard not to smile back.

"Plus, you have a witness." He points to himself. "And I bet those other guys would sell him out in a minute."

I nod, only partly reassured. "I thought I killed him."

"Yeah, the world should be so lucky."

Sam pulls himself up, and since we're still holding hands, I follow. We creep forward. He squints into the sunlight and scans the driveway, the street, the neighborhood. "I think we're okay. Thirsty after all that running?"

He gives me a crooked sort of grin. My mouth goes even dryer than before. All I can do is nod. But we don't move. He drops my hand, but it's only so he can bring his fingertips to my cheek.

"You have some mud," he says. "Right here."

He brushes my skin, and my heart rate doubles. I feel as if I haven't stopped running away from the park. Except now, I feel like I should be racing toward something.

Sam licks his ring finger. Halfway to my face, he freezes. "Uh, do you mind?"

"No." I squeak the word, more mouse than girl. I wonder if I look awful with mud on my face. Then I wonder if that matters at all, not when he touches me.

"There." He grins that crooked grin.

Just as I'm thinking I've never seen such light in his green eyes before, he leans forward. His lips brush mine. Warm. Soft. Quick. *Real.*

"Do you mind?" he whispers.

"No." This time, the word is all air.

"Good." He nods toward the door. "Let's go."

————

INSIDE, he squeezes past a few boxes in the entryway, and I follow. They look like moving boxes, and I glance around. The apartment is small, clean, and bright, and I can't tell if they're coming —or going.

"Are you guys moving?" I ask, part of me dreading the answer.

Sam shrugs. "Who knows?"

We unload our coats and kick off muddy shoes. My socks are soaked. They leave little impressions on the tile. Sam vanishes into a small room that smells like detergent and emerges a moment later with a pair of what are clearly boy socks.

"Here," he says. "I can toss yours in the dryer."

I tug on the socks, not sure I want to hand Sam my wet ones. I wrinkle my nose, but laugh at the face Sam makes when he takes my socks. I leave my cell phone with my jacket but take the script. It's Sam's, after all, even if it is smudged and crinkled.

"Hey, buddy, you home?"

I recognize Sam's dad from all those summers in the park. He's in socks, like we are, and carries an open laptop in one hand. When he sees me, his eyebrows go up a notch.

"We got thirsty," Sam says. "Dad, you remember Jolia, the girl I used to play with at the park right?"

His dad stands back and gives me a long look before saying, "Of course. Good to see you."

"Jolia's in Speech at Fremont," Sam adds. "We're practicing."

His dad continues almost like he hasn't heard him. He has the same dark hair and square jaw as Sam. "How are your parents?"

"Good," I say.

"Tell your dad I read his article in *Wired*. Very impressive."

"I will. He likes it when people actually read what he writes."

Sam's dad laughs. "And your brother—Derek, was it?"

I nod. "He's going to the University of Wisconsin."

"Good school." He leans against the wall like he's settling in for a long conversation, but before he can get too comfortable Sam clears his throat.

"Well." Sam's dad grins at both of us, and I can see the resemblance between father and son. "I'll let you practice then." He hefts the laptop. "Work calls. Drinks in the fridge if you're thirsty."

Sam digs two bottles of soda from the refrigerator while I think of all the questions I probably shouldn't ask, like: *Is it just you and your Dad? Are you moving soon? Is it somewhere far away?* But I sense Sam doesn't want to talk about these things. He rips open a bag of chips, and for a while, the sugar and salt are enough.

At last, he says, "We should practice."

I glance at the scripts on the table and feel my cheeks heat. "I don't get this," I say, "the whole role reversal and different script thing."

"It's to help you relax. It's impossible to be tense if you're having fun."

"I don't think speech can be fun," I say.

"See," he says, standing up. "That's what *I* don't get. You used to be so good at it."

I have no idea what he's talking about. "I've never done speech before."

"Sure you have. All those times in the park, you know." And here, his cheeks color, a quick pink rinse that's gone almost before I can see it. But is it adorable? Oh, yes. Yes, it is.

"That was playing." I can barely force the words from my mouth. "You know, pretend."

"That's what speech is."

I give my head an emphatic shake. "No, it's not. It's nothing like that. That was fun—well, you know, back then, when we were little." Do I sound dumb? I wonder. Yeah, I sound dumb. But I'm smart enough to hold in what I really want to say to him: *Those were some of my favorite days.*

"Speech is exactly that." Sam picks up a script and pages through it. "Why do you think I do it? People hand me awards for doing what little kids do every day."

"You don't get scared?"

"Well, sure." He shrugs and I'm certain he's never felt the fear I have. "But you just use that as fuel."

"You're not afraid someone will laugh at you?"

He gives me a look. "I'm hoping they will."

I laugh, because clearly that's what he wants right then.

"My problem is I want to do everything. I drove my coach crazy last year by switching categories and trying new pieces. This year, she's all: 'Pick two, pick two.'"

By my count, he's done more than two. "Still having problems with that?"

"Yeah." He hangs his head in mock shame. "I am."

He's so joyful about the whole thing. He really does love speech. If only I could capture a tenth of that, maybe speech wouldn't be so bad.

He hands me my script. "Don't think. Just pretend you're Romeo, even though it's silly, okay?"

I nod, grip my script, and wait for my cue. He climbs onto the kitchen table (which I can't believe his dad lets him do) and then heaves a dramatic sigh, his gaze on an invisible moon and stars. Maybe it's the high pitched voice he uses as Juliet, or the fact that my sword is now a soup ladle. I relax. Not all at once. Not completely. Some of the tension melts from my shoulders. The fear inside me thaws.

I feel like spring.

When we finish, applause sounds behind us. I spin, the ladle flying from my hand, striking the kitchen window and landing in the sink.

"That's two points," Sam says.

Sam's dad laughs. "I think that performance—all of it—deserves some pizza." He turns to me. "Jolia, can you stay for dinner?"

I peer at Sam and he nods, like he really wants me to stay. "I'll have to call my parents."

"I'll be glad to talk to them," his dad says. "And afterward, Sam can walk you home."

Sam picks up the phone and hands it to me. I don't know why my fingers tremble when I punch in the number, or my voice shakes when Mom picks up. A nervous flutter fills my stomach, and I'm sure I won't be able to eat any pizza.

Mom says yes, and I hand the phone over to Sam's dad. I turn toward Sam. One look into those summer green eyes and I know.

This is more than just playing in the park. At least for me.

———

I MAKE it through pizza and garlic bread without getting tomato sauce on my shirt or cheese stuck to my chin. It's dark when we finally leave Sam's apartment, and the air feels like winter again. A thin layer of ice crunches beneath my Converse sneakers. Sam's pulled on a matching pair, and I'm trying to act like I haven't noticed this.

"You were really brave today," he says, voice hushed.

"I think you were." My voice is also quiet. It's like we're both scared Crandall is close enough to hear us. "You were trying to stop it. I just froze."

"Yeah, and then you shish-kabobed his bike."

"Do you think—"

"I think it was awesome." Sam laughs. "He so deserved that. I bet no one ever fought back like that before."

I let his praise push the worry to the back of my mind. Crandall doesn't know my name; he doesn't know where I live. I can't decide if I should feel guilty about breaking his bike or glad that it gave us the chance to escape.

"Can I ask you something?" he says.

I nod, although I'm not sure he can see me.

"Were you scared?"

Couldn't he tell? "I was terrified."

"You didn't look it."

Up ahead, my house comes into view. I have a question of my own and not a lot of time to ask it. I swallow hard, then say, "Can I ask you something?"

"Sure."

"Why do they call you Romeo?" I can't believe the words left my mouth, but I want—need—to know what he says, to hear his side of things. I want to make sure this is more than playing in the park for him too. And maybe, just maybe, a small part of me is worried about being played.

"Oh, that." Sam laughs again, but I hear hurt behind it. "It started in ninth grade. My English teacher was taking attendance and called me Romeo instead of Romero. It stuck, especially when we started reading the play. Bad week. Bad timing." He sighs. "Of course it spilled over into the speech team. You couldn't pay me now to do Shakespeare."

My mind goes to the balcony scene we read through all afternoon. "Really?"

He laughs. "I mean, at a tournament. Although, actually, I'd love to."

So would I. Where did that thought come from? I don't know. When this speech season is done, so am I. In fact, I may never talk again.

Our feet crunch ice for a few more steps before he continues.

"And last year, there was this group of girls, at the tournaments, who followed me around. I think it was kind of a joke—you know." He shrugs like this is no big deal, like he can take a joke—or be a joke.

But girls following Sam around makes sense to me. Kaitlin and Savannah can't stop whispering about him, no matter what Tory says. Then I think about what Kaitlin said, how *Tory* followed Sam around. Tory's tough, but she doesn't waste time being deliberately cruel. What's left then? A crush? Amazing how things look so different, depending on what side you stand on.

"I don't think it was a joke," I say. I want to tell him lots of girls like him, but I'm not sure I want him knowing about all those other girls.

"Now, of course, everyone calls me that." Sam rolls his eyes. "You heard them at the awards ceremony."

We stop in front of my driveway. The air grows colder around us, and there isn't a hint of sun left in the sky.

"Thanks," I say, "for walking me home."

"You're not there yet."

So we keep going, up the driveway and the three steps onto the front porch. There, the lamplight turns everything yellow, even Sam's eyes, which look more like autumn than summer right now. I should open the door and go inside. My fingers are ice, my nose threatening to run. My teeth, which I've hardly thought of all day, prick at my upper lip. Insidious words pop into my mind.

Can you even imagine anyone wanting to kiss that? I can't remember why I ever thought she was pretty.

"Thanks for helping me today," I say despite my teeth.

"Thanks for helping me. What did I tell you? It's like the Montagues and Capulets, only with scripts instead of swords—and a tree branch."

I laugh.

"See you tomorrow?"

I nod.

"I'll text you."

We don't move, like earlier in the garage, when it felt like the very air changed. It does that now, becomes hard to breathe. I sway forward, slightly. I don't mean to—it just happens. Sam takes my hands, squeezes them. Then he sways forward.

His kiss is so warm, it should melt all the icicles hanging from the eaves. My heart beats so hard, it should shatter all my ribs. When he breaks the kiss, and I suck in cold air, I feel like I'm plunged from a warm dream into an icy bath.

"Tomorrow!" He dashes down the stairs and into the night.

In that single word, I hear his promise. We will see each other tomorrow. We will practice. We will … kiss?

With a fingertip, I touch my lips and then my teeth. Still there, still where they should be. Still unbelievable.

I push open our front door just as my cell phone buzzes in my coat pocket. My heart hammers. It can't possibly be Sam, but part of me hopes it is. Instead, the text is from Caro.

Caro: WHERE ARE YOU?!!!?

I scroll through what I've missed while at Sam's. Three phone calls and six text messages from Caro, each one more urgent. I've missed Grand Slam, blown Caro's chances of seeing Jeremy until Monday.

All for pizza with Sam. I stare at the screen until it grows dim and finally goes black. I try to type a message, but even my fingertips feel guilty. I don't know what to say, don't know what to type.

So instead, I turn off my phone.

———

DAD WAS RIGHT. Winter is still here. Even inside the lobby entryway, the cold sneaks in, making my tights feel icy against my legs. I'm clutching my bag close, but it doesn't do much to warm me up, even though it's filled with fuzzy yarn.

In the field next to the school, the senior class is taking advantage of the warm up and cool down to start on their snow sculpture for the winter carnival. Every year, our school hosts a huge event with skating and snow sculpture, a bonfire, and lots of hot chocolate. Last year, Caro and I worked on the one for the freshmen class. In the end, Mrs. Sulvana wouldn't let her go because the snowball and couples skate sounded too much like a dance. Which it isn't, but kind of is. I tagged along with Derek and his friends, but it wasn't much fun without Caro.

The bus pulls up and we all troop outside. Another Saturday, another tournament, another chance to see Sam. I'm trying to concentrate on that, and not on what a lousy best friend I am. It's why I have my knitting with me. If I click the needles all the way to the Chisago High School, I won't have to think how Caro hasn't answered a single one of my messages—text, email, or phone.

It almost works. Tory rolls her eyes when I pull out the yarn, a soft dove gray that I'm combining with a steel blue. The colors are very school uniform, but in a good way. I'm thinking it will be perfect to wear when I read *Jane Eyre*. Savannah and Kaitlin sit behind me. Their questions pepper the back of my head.

"Is it hard?"

"When did you learn?"

"Can you teach me?"

"You guys can join the knitting club," I say. "Every Tuesday morning at seven forty-five. You can be an absolute beginner. It doesn't matter. Caro only started last year." The second I say this, I immediately regret it. Maybe I should use the bus ride to review her messages, try to find a way to apologize. But part of me insists I already did that last night and then some. And maybe I don't really have anything to apologize for. I go back to knitting.

"We should," Savannah says.

"Oh, me, too," Ryan pipes in. "I want to learn to knit."

Kaitlin and Savannah giggle. I simply say, "Guys knit. In fact, we have a couple of guys in the club."

Ryan snorts.

"Probably because there are so many girls in the club," I add.

Ryan leans forward in full flirt mode, and Tory smacks him on the arm.

"Focus," she says. "You can play around after the season is over."

It's painfully obvious I don't want to be on the speech team. I'm sure that's clear to Tory. But Ryan? For the first time I wonder how much he wants to be here.

When we arrive at Chisago High School, it feels colder than when we left. Ben scoops up some snow, tries to pack it into a ball, but it crunches and crumbles in his fingers. Inside, we crowd around a cafeteria table, like always. The air is full of jittery static, everyone's nervousness rising toward the ceiling. My cell phone buzzes in my skirt pocket, and I slip it out, oh, so casually.

Sam: 28

I get my room assignments, pick up my script and bottle of water, and head off in search of room 28. It's not far from the cafeteria, and I worry that we're too close to his team and mine. But I figure Sam knows what he's doing.

"Hey," he says when I ease the door closed behind me.

"Hey."

Then, we stand there. It's dorky and awkward and somehow, not.

"Yesterday was great," I say.

"Yeah, it was."

"I mean, dinner at your place, not the part where I almost killed Crandall."

"No, that part was pretty good, too."

I laugh.

"Want to run through your piece a few times?"

I sigh. "Do I want to? No. Should I? Probably."

Now Sam laughs. His eyes are filled with so much light today, like everything he sees makes him happy.

"Just a few times," he says. "Get you all warmed up for your rounds."

So I begin. When I reach the part where Mr. Brocklehurst forces Jane to stand on the stool, Sam stops me.

"You know what? You should try to find someone in your real life who can be a stand-in for Brocklehurst. It might help you give this part of the scene more emotional resonance."

I glance around the room as if that person might be sitting in one of the desks. "I don't know. Maybe Mr. Henderson?"

"Seriously?" Sam's brow wrinkles. "He seems like a pretty good guy to me."

That's because Mr. Henderson would love to have Sam on his speech team. He does not love having me on the team, and the feeling is mutual.

Sam peers up at the clock. "We should probably head out."

I nod, but don't move. When he reaches the front of the room, his hand finds its way to mine. I swear that's how it works, and together we sneak toward the door. He switches off the light.

"I'll check," he says. "Make sure the coast is clear."

In the dark, my breathing sounds louder. The room is gloomy in the half light, and we inch closer to each other. My pulse beats in my throat as the door creaks open. But the kiss on my lips is soft and sweet—like hot chocolate.

"Good luck today," he whispers into my mouth.

He swings the door open and we both bolt from the room.

———————

DURING MY LAST ROUND, something clicks. Before I open my mouth to speak, I glance at the clock. A shockwave rushes through me. Yesterday, Sam and I were in the park. Yesterday, I put a tree branch through Crandall's front tire. My stomach flip flops. My heart races. I lick my lips, but only once, before I speak. Sam's advice fills my head. It's perfectly right, but my thinking is all wrong. Mr. Henderson is strict and kind of prickly, but he's no bully. Crandall on the other hand? Did Jane feel trapped on that stool the way I did yesterday?

I realize there are worse things than speaking in front of a group or even being laughed at. I channel everything I felt yesterday into today. When I say Brocklehurst, I imagine Crandall.

I'd never tasted fear like that—the certainty that something terrible would happen. I never want to taste that fear again. But since there's so much of it in my mouth, I know it must lace my words.

After the third round, I'm feeling bouncy. I almost skip back to the cafeteria. When I notice they've already posted some of the scores, I skitter to a stop. Then I inch forward as if scuffling the linoleum with my ballet flats changes what's printed on the paper.

Prose is posted. Already. For a long time, I stare, not certain what I see is real. My phone buzzes in my pocket.

Sam: Well?

I peck out the numbers slowly, sending each one in its own text.

5

4

3

Sam: That's a flush! You're doing it!

Am I? Am I really? Before I can text Sam back, Tory bustles by. I shove my phone into my pocket so hard, I nearly tear the seam. She halts, backs up, and stares at the prose scores. Then, she turns her gaze on me.

"Seriously?" she says.

I shrug. "I guess."

"Huh. What do you know?" She gives me one last look, one that hints that I might not be completely unworthy, before continuing down the hall.

Chapter 9

THE LENS of Tory's digital camera is aimed straight at my face. The camera sits on a tripod, and that perches on a table, and the whole thing teeters. Any second now and none of us will have to worry about recording our pieces.

I feel like Jane on her stool, trapped again, and I try to channel that feeling, using it for fuel, like Sam talked about. I ignore the donkey teeth and try not to trip over my tongue.

When I finish, Tory clicks the camera off and then stares at me.

"Not bad," she says. "You're tapping into something you haven't before. No wonder your scores improved. You know what you should do?"

I shake my head, still mulling what *not bad* means.

"Read your piece into the bathroom mirror at home, only place a pencil like this." She shoves a pencil in her mouth so she clenches it against her molars. She looks like a dog with a very yellow, very skinny bone. "It does wonders for your pronunciation," she says around the pencil.

"It doesn't sound like it."

She spits the pencil onto the floor, then laughs. "After you take it out, during your rounds. Trust me." She fiddles with the camera, switching the settings to play. "Want to see how you did?"

It's not a question, even though it sounds like one. "Not really."

"It won't be that awful."

It is that awful. I cover my face with my hands and watch the recording through the V made by my fingers.

"Right here." Tory pauses the video. "Near the end, when you're all Jane on her stool? Something's different." She scrutinizes me. "Whatever you're doing, keep it up."

My mind goes to Sam and our secret practices, and it's all I can do not to smile.

At last, Tory lets me sit and calls up Kaitlin, who does poetry interpretation. I slide into my seat next to Savannah.

"Not bad," she says to me.

I've been so awful that "not bad" feels like a major accomplishment. I think of my failing speech grade and decide that "not bad" could be much, much worse.

Savannah goes back to fretting over her piece, marking places in the text for emphasis and emotion. I slip my cell phone from my pocket and scroll through this weekend's text messages.

Before Caro's message of: WHERE ARE YOU, she sent:

Grand Slam. Mom said yes!!!! Call me!

Do you want to go? Pleeze!

Hey, pick up your phone.

Mom says if you don't answer in 30 min, Grand Slam is a NO!

5 more minutes. J, pleasepleasepleaseplease!

Caro still isn't speaking to me. I tried all day Sunday with no luck. I'm dying to tell her about Sam—except he's the reason she couldn't see Jeremy over the long weekend. There's no winning that conversation.

I sigh and hide my phone just as Ryan invades our table. He lands in a chair, taking up enough space for two people. Savannah shifts her script so he won't crumple it.

"Henderson is moving me over to prose."

"Does that make you a P&P girl?" I ask.

Savannah giggles.

Ryan ignores me and shuffles the pages of his own script, looking less than enthused about it—or us. It's hard to tell. "We heard that Winnetka is pulling Romero from prose. He'll be doing great speeches and maybe something else—no one's sure about that."

My stomach flutters. Sam? Not in prose? "How do you guys hear about this stuff?"

"Oh, we have our ways." Ryan crosses his arms over his chest, a superior expression on his face.

Savannah glances at me and rolls her eyes. I want to do the same, but I need to stay on Ryan's good side. How do they know such things? Do they have a spy? And if they do, what if this spy sees me with Sam?

"No, really," I say. "How do you guys find out?"

Ryan leans back in his chair, hands clasped behind his head, his eyes half-lidded, like he knows all sorts of things we don't.

"It's like poker," Savannah says.

He sits up, and his face goes blank, but I get what she's saying. It's like each team is bluffing the other.

"Or chess." I plunk invisible chess pieces across the table. "The Winnetka coach moves one speaker here, Mr. Henderson moves you there."

"It's not like that," Ryan says.

"Yeah? Then why are you doing prose?" I ask. "Do you want to?"

"It's okay." He stares down at his script and straightens the pages. "Henderson didn't like my intro."

"So he sent you over here to the bad kid corner?" Savannah says.

I laugh. Ryan doesn't.

"What are you doing?" I ask.

"*Unbroken* by Laura Hillenbrand. I wrote this great intro, but Henderson says it doesn't fit the piece."

"Can I see your script?" I hold out my hand.

He gives me a quizzical look but passes me the pages. I read the intro, then flip through the scene he selected. Dad is a big World War Two buff. I gave him the book for Christmas, then read it right after he did. It's some pretty serious stuff, about a bombardier whose plane is shot down over the Pacific Ocean. First he survives in the ocean, then a Japanese prisoner of war camp. There are lots of scenes Ryan could be reading for his piece, and the intro should be a snap to write.

"Well," I say to him. "Your piece isn't about fear. That's your problem."

"Huh?"

"It's about courage."

"Are you kidding me?" He bolts straight up. "They're scared to death."

The scene he picked involves a raft in the middle of the Pacific Ocean, and yes, all three men are scared. But two of them act—and that's the whole point.

"Make it about acting despite being scared," I say. "There's a lot of reasons the book is called *Unbroken*." I tap his script. "This is just one of them. Have you read the whole thing?"

Ryan's cheeks go pink. "Well, you know, I started to—"

"Not bad advice, Ms. Cuppernull."

We all jump. Mr. Henderson towers over us as if he's suddenly appeared from nowhere. Savannah's eyes go wide, and even Ryan goes a little pale.

"Maybe you should write everyone's introductions." This doesn't sound like sarcasm. It sounds almost like a compliment.

Mr. Henderson walks away, and Ryan looks at me like my words drip with gold—or at least, the gold paint that covers all the trophies.

"You should Google for courage quotes," I tell him.

He nudges his script closer to me. "What else would you do?"

I wonder what on earth has happened. Then I think: that's it. I'm not *on* Earth. I can't be. I'm on some planet where I can actually help the co-captain of the speech team, a planet where I'm not completely bad at speech.

———

ALL WEEK LONG, lunch is weird and silent. I still sit next to Caro, but an invisible wall has sprung up between us. She leans toward Jeremy, chin planted on her hand, like she's totally absorbed in all the jock talk. More than once, her eyelids droop. I think she might tip over and crash onto the floor from boredom.

After school, she heads out into the snow to help build the sophomore class sculpture for the winter carnival. If not for speech, I'd be there too—for all the good it would do me. Indoors or out, things are icy with Caro.

This is why, on Wednesday night, when my phone rings, my fingers can't quite move fast enough to answer. I drop the phone. I pick it up. I almost disconnect the call. Then I see it isn't Caro.

It's Sam.

Sam.

"Hey," he says when I finally remember how to use all my limbs and answer the phone.

"Hey."

I think this will be the extent of our conversation when Sam continues, like he doesn't have to think twice about this talking thing.

"You know, I was thinking about your scores on Saturday," he says.

"Yeah, you and Tory."

"Oh, so she noticed too. Good sign."

"If you say so."

"I do. Anyway, I'm thinking we get in an extra practice this week. That might really help. Are you free tomorrow night? We could meet at the library and use one of their study rooms."

I would so love to be free tomorrow night. Normally I would be, but the orchestra has its mid-season concert that night.

"I can't miss it," I tell him. "It's part of our grade."

"Could I go?" he asks.

"You want to go to a high school orchestra concert?"

"I like music."

"It's not like I have a solo or anything. I mean, it's just ... I don't know." Is it weird he wants to go to something some parents don't even want to attend?

"Would you mind?" he asks.

It hits me then. I don't mind. In fact, Sam, seeing me do something I'm good at? All of a sudden, I want him there.

"No. I don't mind."

"Great. So it's—"

"Seven thirty, Fremont High auditorium. I'll be the girl with the violin."

The next day, I barely notice the deep freeze from Caro. I don't even notice if she notices that I'm somewhere else during lunch. Once or twice, I pluck the strings on an invisible violin and sigh. I can't decide if tonight will be the best thing ever or a horrible mistake that I'll regret for the rest of my life.

That night, after I slip into my formal concert dress, Mom pulls my hair back with a black satin headband (so it won't fall into my eyes when I play) and then curls the ends. I pray my hair will stay curled, at least until Sam can see it.

Problem is, I don't see Sam in the auditorium. Of course, with the house lights down and the stage lights in my eyes, there's not much I can see except my sheet music.

For an hour, I don't think about Sam—or at least, not that much. It's all about the music. I love playing my violin. I don't even mind being up on stage. I'm not Jane on her stool, I'm Jolia in a chair, and I'm not alone.

Afterwards, I lock my violin in its cubby and hurry into the hallway where parents and friends wait. And there, standing with Mom and Dad, is Sam. His eyes go wide when he sees me.

"Whoa," he says. "You look great."

Okay, so my concert formal is fancy, but it's not like a prom dress or anything. The top is velvet, but with long sleeves. It has an empire waist and something Mom calls a chiffon overlay, but I'm not entirely certain what that means. Still. The way Sam is looking at me? I'm so glad Mom curled my hair.

"You didn't tell me you played in the fancy orchestra," he says.

Fremont High has two orchestras, the philharmonic, which I play in, and symphony strings, which is where you play if you don't want to try out for the philharmonic.

I shrug. "Anyone can, with enough practice."

Sam nudges me in the ribs. "Kind of like speech, huh?"

I ignore this.

Around us, girls from orchestra are giving me sidelong glances. Some are simply staring at Sam. Of course, he is really cute, and he doesn't go to our school. I catch sight of a senior girl throwing her arms around her boyfriend's neck, and a flash of warmth washes over my cheeks. That's what this looks like. Sam. Me.

He's my ... boyfriend?

"Hey," Dad says. "Who's up for some ice cream? Sam? Want to come along? We can give you a lift home."

"I don't have regular clothes," I say.

"That's okay." There's a hint of a smile on Sam's face.

He calls his dad, and within a minute, we're all in the car, heading for Sonnies Ice Cream Parlor. Still, a concert formal at an ice cream place?

"I feel like a dork," I whisper to Sam when we walk inside.

"But a pretty dork."

My stomach jumps, both at his words and at the fact that we're out, together, where someone from the Winnetka or Fremont speech teams might see us. Is this really a good idea? I cast him a glance, then survey the tables. No one looks familiar, but then I don't know everyone on the Winnetka team.

But if Sam isn't worried, then I shouldn't be either. We decide to split a hot fudge sundae. He's balancing it in both hands when Mom says, "Oh, look, why don't you two take that little table over there."

"Why don't we get a booth," Dad counters. "I want to talk to Sam about running."

Mom takes Dad by the shoulder and directs him away from me and Sam. If it weren't so humiliating, I might actually laugh. As it is, we do get our table for two.

"So," Sam says, between spoonsful of hot fudge. "The violin?"

"It lets me think. So does knitting."

"What do you think about?"

Lately? Sam. Normally? "Well, stories, actually."

"Stories?"

"I … think them up, work the plot out in my head." I explain about the graphic novel Caro and I plan to work on during creative storytelling. I even manage to do this without worrying too much about the fact Caro isn't talking to me.

"A modern retelling of *Romeo and Juliet*?" Sam grins.

"Yeah, I know. It's been done, but Caro really wanted to do it."

"Why not? I mean, didn't they make a version with garden gnomes?"

"They did!"

"You could ... I don't know, use speech teams or something."

I laugh.

"Are you going to change the ending?" he asks.

I tip my head, considering this. "Caro wants to."

"But you're not so sure."

I pick up my scarf that's coiled next to me. "I'm still trying to work it out." I poke my fingers between a couple of stitches I dropped and didn't realize it until too late. "See? Plot holes."

"You know what you should do, I mean, in speech next year?"

"I think you're assuming I'll be in speech next year," I say.

"No, listen." He leans forward, those green eyes so intent on mine. "Storytelling." He goes on to explain how you draw a selection of folktales, decide on one, reinterpret it, and then perform it that day—all without a script.

I shake my head, appalled he'd suggest such a thing. "It's like the extemporaneous speaking Tory does."

"Only more fun and more creative."

Maybe, but why he thinks I'd be good at it is beyond me.

On the way home, Mom drives so Dad can spin around in the front seat and bombard Sam with running, running shoe, and every other kind of question related to running—none of which seems to annoy Sam. He could probably do an extemporaneous speech on the merit of shoes and running and make it sound halfway interesting.

When Mom pulls up in front of Sam's apartment, Dad is still spun around, staring at us. We're all frozen like that. I wonder what it is we're expecting. Then Mom taps Dad on the shoulder.

"Oh, look, honey," she says. "A deer."

Dad swivels around at the same moment Sam leans close and

gives my cheek a quick kiss. He bursts from the car like his coat is on fire. Then it's just me, Mom, Dad, and a whole lot of awkward in the backseat.

"So," Mom says. "Sam Romero. Anything we should know?"

"We're both in speech." I'm certain this is not what she means.

Mom puts the car in gear. "And?"

"I don't know?"

"Well," she says, voice all sly. "I think Sam knows."

"Knows what?" Dad asks.

Mom sighs. But when I catch her glance in the rearview mirror, I swear she winks at me.

———

THAT SATURDAY, I'm missing Caro so much, when I reach the spot in my script where Helen Burns smiles at Jane, my throat gets tight. I finish up, gulp a breath, and wait for Sam's verdict.

"Nice," he says. "The Brocklehurst emotion is really starting to show. And the connection with Helen and Jane." He pauses as if considering the entire performance. "You're looking at higher scores this time."

I don't say anything.

"You don't see it, do you?"

I shake my head.

"Just wait." He seems so certain.

Like last week, at the end of practice, Sam snaps off the lights and then eases the door open. Only this time, he flings himself back inside. We huddle against the wall, breathe in quick, shallow breaths.

"Who was it?" I ask.

"Some girls from my team."

Girls who follow him around? I wonder, then order myself not to do that crazy girlfriend thing. Because, one, as far as I know, I am not Sam's girlfriend. And two, no one likes the crazy.

We wait in the dark and I try not to think crazy thoughts.

"It's kind of like being secret agents," he says.

Okay, that is crazy, but a good kind of crazy. I grin. "I was thinking the same thing," I say, although, really, I wasn't.

He puts a hand on the doorknob, but freezes. "Hey, some of us Winnetka guys are thinking about crashing the winter carnival."

They can't really crash it since it's outdoors and open to everyone, but I know what he means.

"You going to be there?" he asks.

"I don't know. I—I think so."

"Maybe I'll see you there. Do you skate?"

"A little."

"Like you play the violin a little."

"No, not like that."

"You're probably better than me. You'll have to prop me up during the snowball skate."

I will? Before I can respond, Sam cracks open the door. "It's all clear."

I feel the world's fastest kiss on my cheek. There's no time for wishing luck or saying goodbye. We dash from the room. He heads one way, I go the other. I don't think anything of water running in the girls' bathroom, but when I hit the stairs I teeter on the top step, just for a moment, and glance behind.

Nothing. All clear. I race for my first round, thinking of Sam's praise, the kiss on my cheek, and the promise of the winter carnival.

———

THE FIRST ROUND has started and advice crowds my head. I think about how Sam tells me to pretend, to channel emotion. I think about what Tory said, about being all Jane on her stool. That sums it up perfectly. Every time I stand in front of a group, I think of that and not my teeth. I don't know if I'm getting any better, but I do know this: I'm not any worse.

After the third round, I clear the door to the cafeteria when the phone in my skirt pocket vibrates.

Sam: Checked your scores?

Jolia: No.

Sam: GO! CHECK!

I spin around and head down the hall. It's easy to see where the scores are posted. A bunch of kids swarm around one of the walls, ducking in and out and under arms. I join in, pushing my way toward the prose interpretation list.

I bump Savannah, who gives my arm a quick squeeze before she dashes off. I find prose and track the names in reverse alphabetical order. I see *Dinsmore, Ryan* with an iffy score of 2, 2, 3. I wonder if Mr. Henderson will pull him from prose and have him try something else.

Then I see my scores and forget all about Ryan.

3, 3, 3

No fives? Not even a four? I'm perfectly average? I do a quick check of the finalist lists, confirming that yes, Tory double finaled again—and so did Sam. I escape to the far side of the hall and pull out my cell.

Jolia: 3, 3, 3!!!!!

Sam: You can do better.

Jolia: I don't need to do better.

When it comes to speech, I can't imagine asking for more than average. If I do well on my persuasive and how-to speeches in class, I will pull off a solid C. I can stay in the honors program. I will get to write my graphic novel, assuming Caro starts speaking to me again.

Sam: But you can do better.

I ignore that.

Jolia: What final do you want me to watch?

Unlike kids who double final, spectators can't slip in and out of the final rounds—it's rude and disruptive. I'll have to pick one and stick with it.

Sam: Great speeches. My speech is really ... great.

I laugh. The great speeches final is right across the hall from the prose final round. No one says anything when I slip into the wrong room at the last minute.

Besides, didn't Tory want us to keep an eye on Romeo Romero? Well, here I am, keeping a very close eye on him. Still, the tiniest bit of guilt chips away at my happiness. Who do I support? My team? Or the boy who wears weeds in his hair for me?

But when I'm there in great speeches, chin resting on my hand, gazing up at Sam, I know I've made my choice.

I just hope it's the right one.

———

WE'RE WAITING for the awards ceremony to begin when the Winnetka girls find us. At first, I don't notice. I'm too busy thinking about both Sam and Caro. I'm so excited about my performance today, so blown away by Sam's in great speeches, I just know I can craft the perfect text message to Caro—the one that will make her laugh and text me back. I've just pulled out my phone when the Winnetka girls march up the aisle.

While I don't really know any of them, I can tell they're coming straight for us. They're all suited up, like clones of Tory. But Tory is clearly unimpressed. She wrinkles her nose, then turns her back on them.

The Winnetka girls keep coming. They file into the row beneath ours and stop right in front of me.

"We know what you're doing," the one in the middle says. She's also the one who looks the most like a Tory clone, right down to her hair pulled into a bun.

"Yeah." Tory spins around. "We're trouncing you."

"No." The girl points at me. "With her."

Tory slants a quick look my way, then studies the girl in front of her. "Huh?"

"We know *all* about it," the girl says. "And you're not going to get away with it."

My insides go cold. I hold still and hold in all the fear that's filled my mouth. I think back to the water running in the girls' bathroom—and before, when the Winnetka girls were in the hallway. Or maybe it started even earlier, at Sonnies?

Tory mimics feeling the girl's forehead, but the Winnetka girl pulls away before Tory can touch her. "I think the stress of competition is getting to you, Annika," Tory says. "Maybe you should join the knitting club."

Ouch. I pluck at the sweater vest I'm wearing—the one I made myself—but Tory doesn't notice.

"We know *why* she's a new member this year," the Winnetka girl says.

Tory gapes at them. My heart stops, then pounds so hard in my chest, my ribcage aches with it. They know I'm failing speech class? How could they? None of this makes any sense. From the expression on Tory's face, I can tell she feels the same way.

"Just so you know," Annika says as she and the other two shuffle from the row and into the aisle. "We're not going to let you get away with it."

For a few seconds, we're all silent. Kaitlin and Savannah stare with huge eyes. Fear tightens the back of my throat. I want to speak, but I'm not sure how to explain or even where to start.

"I think their coach is working them too hard." Tory makes a face. "They're crazier than usual this year." She laughs, loud enough that Annika glances over. "And jealous," Tory adds.

"Jealous?" I ask.

"Yeah, of you."

"Me?"

"All the Winnetka boys think you're hot."

They do? They do!

"Don't let it go to your head. It's just because you're new." Tory sniffs, clearly as unimpressed with Winnetka boys as she is with the girls. "Next year, it will be someone else."

Oh. Not that I really care. There's only one Winnetka boy who matters. I ease into my seat and glance toward the Winnetka team, hoping to see Sam. Instead, the Winnetka girls glare at me. I jerk my head toward the stage, pretending to be absorbed in the trophy setup, pretending that what they said doesn't matter. But deep down, I'm afraid everything they said does matter—I just don't know how.

———

ON THE BUS ride back to Fremont, my phone buzzes. I glance around, wary. What if it's Sam? Not that anyone can see my display. Still. It's one thing to fraternize with the enemy, as Tory would say. It's another to have him—virtually—on the bus. Slowly, I peek at my phone. Not Sam, but my heart thumps hard anyway. *Caro.*

She's sent me a message, and my fingers hit the wrong key when I try to read it. At last, I bring it up.

Caro: OmigodOmigodOmigod.

Jolia: What? What?

Caro: Mom said YES!!!!!

Before I can ask to what, another message arrives.

Caro: I can go to the winter carnival!!!!!

The news stuns me. She can go? I can't believe it or get my fingers to peck out a reply.

Caro: Do you want to go?

Just five words. That's all. But I can read the apology in them. We're friends again. It's the perfect ending to my perfectly average wonderful day. I type in the only thing I can and hit send.

Jolia: Of course.

Chapter 10

ALL WEEK AT LUNCH, Caro and I talk about the winter carnival. I bring in a scarf I've knitted on the sly. It's a dark pink paired with moss green, in fun fur, of course, since it's for Caro. It doesn't look like a little kid's scarf, even with the pink, and the color makes her olive skin glow. She surprises me with a knitted headband, the first thing she's knitted on her own without any help.

"It's awesome," I say.

"It's not that good."

"It is. I'm totally wearing it on Friday." I won't have to wear a hat then. Caro's curls look great peeking out from beneath a cap. My hair? Not so much. Normally, I wouldn't care—except if Sam's there. Well, I hate to say it, but then I'll care a lot.

I'm so preoccupied by all this that I almost forget to be nervous when it's my turn to give my persuasive speech in Mr. Henderson's class. Almost. I push back the feeling of the donkey teeth by sticking a pencil in my mouth à la Tory a few minutes before it's my turn to speak. It's like a bridle, and since my teeth have a very horse-like quality to them—at least in my mind—I figure why not rein them in.

My speech is all about why you should read classic literature. My reasons range from understanding song lyrics to getting the jokes on The Simpsons. Mr. Henderson actually laughs. My scores resemble the ones from the tournament. All threes out of fives. I am perfectly average, once again, and perfectly happy to be so until Mr. Henderson taps my desk to get my attention.

"I think, Ms. Cuppernull," he says, "that you're capable of doing better."

It's almost like he and Sam are conspiring against me. All I do is nod.

———

FRIDAY CAN'T COME SOON ENOUGH, at least not for Caro. I'm excited, too, but I've been to the winter carnival before. Of course, now, I won't be the tagalong little sister, and we're going to have the best time. I think this right up until Mrs. Sulvana drops us off at the entrance to the snow sculpture display and we walk inside to her cries of, "Eleven thirty, no later!"

I study our class sculpture, a huge version of our school mascot —the falcon. In the dark, it looks menacing and not at all like five year olds went crazy with gallons of paint. The air feels crisp against my eyes and bites my cheeks. But it's not so cold that Mom insisted I wear a hat instead of the headband Caro made me. The soft yarn warms my ears and with enough skating, I won't be cold at all. And if we end up frozen, there's always the bonfire. Of course, I've forgotten the true forecast right up until Caro squeals.

It's cloudy with a one hundred percent chance of Jeremy.

He whirls her around, her boots nearly taking me out at the knees. She's breathless and woozy and grabs onto my coat to steady herself.

"What should we do first?" she asks.

"I thought we came here to skate," Jeremy says.

Caro claps her hands together, then gives me puppy-dog eyes. "Do you mind?"

I hate being ditched every single time we go out with Jeremy. At the same time, I know this means a lot to her. So I smile, shake my head, and wave them off. But part of me wishes I'd said, yes, I mind. I mind a lot. I want to get hot chocolate. I want to inhale its warmth combined with that from the fire—all smoke and chocolate, cold and heat. I want to skate without it having to be a snowball or couples skate. I want do something that doesn't revolve around Jeremy and what he wants.

But of course, I'll never say that. I worry that it makes me, I don't know what, too possessive? Too self-centered? I sigh, wondering what to do when a voice sounds behind me.

"Does she do that all the time?"

I whirl to find Tory standing behind me.

"Do what?" I ask.

"Does she always ditch you for Spinner?"

I shrug. "Her mom ..." I break off, not wanting to rat out Caro. "I mean, it's complicated."

"It's complicated is a Facebook status." Tory's gaze goes to where Caro and Jeremy have vanished through the doors of the warming hut. "That's just mean."

I don't know this side of Tory. Why does she care about Caro? Why is she here, talking to me? Then, words stream from my mouth. I speak on instinct, and I don't even know what I'm going to say until I say it.

"Want to get some hot chocolate or something?"

She stares at me so long, I wonder if my instincts are totally off. I haven't felt the donkey teeth all day, but now I do. I'm certain Tory sees them. When a slow smile spreads across her face, I feel my own mouth go back to normal. Then, I smile too.

"Sure," she says.

At the stand, Tory gets an apple cider. I go for the hot chocolate, and since the guy working the booth knows Derek from swim team, he smothers the top with whipped cream.

"I guess it's good to know people," Tory says.

"You know people."

The silence that follows makes me wonder how true that is. I glance around, searching for the one person who is almost always at Tory's side.

"He's skating already," she says, as if she knows I'm looking for Ryan. "He's showing off, getting warmed up for the snowball skate."

"Do you skate?"

She shrugs.

"Kind of like me on speech team?"

Tory sputters, spitting a mouthful of cider onto the snow. Then she laughs so hard, I'm afraid she might choke.

"I'm …" but she's laughing too hard to finish.

"Better? Worse? About the same?"

"Let's just say Ryan skates a whole lot better than I do."

We head for the warming hut and the rental skates, which are actually free. I haven't been on skates since last year's winter carnival. For the first few times around the rink, I'm as shaky as Tory, who's all arms-outstretched, with the choppy strides of a toddler.

But my legs soon remember what to do, and then I'm skating circles around Tory, not to show off, but so we can still skate together.

"Go," she tells me. "Just say 'hey' each time you lap me."

"I just want to go fast for a bit. I'll be back."

She gives me a *whatever* sort of look and goes back to tottering across the ice.

I skate fast enough that cold stings my eyes. Icy air fills my lungs, but it makes me feel alive, that I might be able to do

106

anything. I weave between skaters, keeping an eye out for Sam. Everyone is so bundled up, sometimes I don't recognize someone I know until I've nearly shot past them.

"Hey!" somebody calls. That somebody is Ryan. He grabs my hands and spins me in a circle.

"You can skate!" he shouts.

"Sort of."

"Better than Tory."

"Be nice," I say.

"Why? She never is."

I'm not so sure how true that is, either. I let my fingers go slack in my mittens. They slip from my hands and Ryan goes stumbling backward. Then he cuts circles around me in a game of keep away.

"Give them back," I say. "My hands are freezing."

Finally, he does. "See you for the snowball skate?" he says.

"Maybe."

He tears off, chasing down two bundled forms that resemble Kaitlin and Savannah. I'm on my own again, wondering why I don't go skating more often. Well, I almost wonder. I know the reason. When I was ten, I begged Mom and Dad for ice skates for Christmas. For the first few days of winter break, I skated until my legs went all noodlely, and I grew blisters on my blisters.

The second week, I slung my skates over my shoulder, tromped through the snow, and found the ice covered with rink rats. That day, I skated along the edges, but I didn't stay long. Then I pleaded with Derek to come with me. Sometimes he did, and sometimes he didn't.

And now? I can't believe I let someone like a rink rat keep me from something I loved. The thought slows my stride, so I'm merely coasting when, over the loudspeaker, the DJ's voice blasts across the ice.

"Okay, everyone, time for the snowball skate. Girls on the end by the warming hut, boys on the other. Find a partner and snowball!"

I'm not sure if I want to stick around for the snowball skate. Across the rink, I see Caro and Jeremy glide into the center, one of the first couples to do so. I know they won't be switching, either, when the DJ calls snowball again.

In a way, Mrs. Sulvana is right about the whole snowball/couples skate. It's a total ramp up for prom. Last year, Derek wanted to ask a girl, but she spent the entire time skating with one of his (not-so-nice) friends. And then this (not-so-nice) friend dumped her the week before prom. Derek offered to go with her, but she was so upset, she turned him down.

"Snowball!" the DJ calls.

Except for the couple-couples, everyone splits off. I'm heading for the bank and the warming hut when Ryan swoops by.

"Hey, you promised!"

Actually, I didn't, but take his hand anyway. He pulls me onto the ice and we zoom around the other couples.

"What's the deal with Caro and Spinner?" he asks.

I peek over my shoulder. Yes, they are still skating together. I shake my head.

"He's kind of a tool," Ryan adds.

I press my lips together, vowing I will not diss my best friend's boyfriend. But it's really, really hard, especially when he nudges me and says, "You think it too."

I say nothing, but I make a face that has Ryan bursting out laughing.

"So, hey, what do you think?" he says. "Couples skate. Kaitlin or Savannah?"

"They're not my type."

"Ha, ha. Seriously. Does either one like me?"

They *both* like him. That's the problem. I don't know what to say to this. Is one a better sport? Does one like him more than the other? I scan the rink. Kaitlin is skating with Ben, who is acting all goofy. I don't see Savannah.

Before I can give Ryan an answer, the DJ calls, "Snowball!"

He doesn't even bother to skate me to the girls' side. He just lets go of my hand. "See ya!"

I coast, but not for long. Someone grabs my hand. I jump, part startled, part hopeful. I turn, hoping for Sam. But it's only Ben.

"I asked Tory to skate," he says, "but it looked like she was about to clobber me."

"She doesn't skate very well."

"That doesn't matter."

Maybe not, but I suspect it matters to Tory. I'm still skating with Ben when the DJ announces it's time for the couples' skate.

"Okay, find that special someone and skate the last song of the night with them."

Ben and I are inching to a stop when Ryan careens past. He does a classic hockey stop in front of Kaitlin and Savannah, kicking up lots of ice flakes. He holds out a hand. From where I'm standing, I can't tell if it's for Kaitlin or Savannah. But when Kaitlin skates off with him, it's clear someone's made a choice.

Savannah's mouth is slack. She pushes a mittened hand across one cheek, then the other.

"Oh, man," Ben says. He turns to me. "Do you mind if I go do a little rescuing?"

"Go. That would be nice."

"I'm not just being nice." He grins at me and skates off.

Now I really am alone in couple world. I heave a sigh, feeling foolish for wishing on Sam all night. Maybe he couldn't get a ride, or his plans changed. I'll see him tomorrow—unless he's sick.

Or not.

What I notice first is the knit cap and a dark fringe of bangs. His legs are wobbly. He really can't skate, and I will have to prop him up. But because this is Sam, and he's making his shaky way toward me, I won't mind at all.

But behind Sam, towering over the skaters, hands on hips, headscarf firmly in place is Caro's mom. I don't think she's seen Caro, not yet. Mrs. Sulvana jerks her head, this way and that, the way you do when you can't find who you're looking for.

And if Mrs. Sulvana does find Caro? My insides match the ice my skates glide over. I can't let this happen. I dart a glance toward Sam who could really use my help. I can't let him down. I can't, I can't, I can't.

What can I do?

Sam is a mere foot away when I spin. It's a show off sort of move—the only one I can really do. The momentum whirls me into him. He staggers backward and lands right on his butt. I bolt past him without a word, without offering him my hand, with barely a look. But I see the disbelief in his eyes.

The hurt. The humiliation. I hear someone laugh, and it's a cold sound. My cheeks heat in response. I don't know how I'm going to explain this to Sam. But it's too late now. I crash into Jeremy and Caro, gripping them both by their jackets. All three of us stagger then right ourselves.

"What the hell?" Jeremy says.

"Your mom," I say to Caro.

"What?" She jerks around, and in that moment, looks oddly like her own mother. "Crap."

I push her toward the warming hut. "Go take off your skates. I'll tell her you went for hot chocolate. By the time she gets back, she won't know the difference."

"God, you're the best."

She skates off. I swivel, hoping my body is enough to block Mrs. Sulvana's view. When Caro clears the snow bank, I hold out my hand to Jeremy. His face scrunches like I'm offering him frozen roadkill.

I don't drop my hand.

"What?" he says.

"This is couples' skate. We need to skate. It's what couples do."

Again with the face.

"Do you want to keep seeing Caro?" I ask. "If not, just stand there."

He takes my hand.

When we skate past Mrs. Sulvana, she gives us a look to melt all the ice.

"Jolia! Jolia!" she calls out. "Have you seen Caro?"

"She was cold," I say. "She went to get some hot chocolate."

"It is late," she says. "We need to leave."

"Yes, ma'am."

She nods once, but the look she sends Jeremy should melt not just the ice, but his skates as well.

"I will see you at the car." With that, she marches off toward the drink booth.

———

THE RIDE HOME IS ICY, both inside the car and out. Tiny snowflakes batter the windshield and the thump of the wipers matches my heartbeat.

"So, this boy," Mrs. Sulvana says. "He's some sort of friend of yours?"

Even with the dark, I see Caro's expression go carefully blank. She looks so impossibly innocent that I'm surprised Mrs. Sulvana doesn't assume she's guilty.

"He's my friend, Mrs. Sulvana," I say before Caro has a chance to speak. I want to say I know him from speech team, but that's something Mrs. Sulvana can check—she's very involved as a parent volunteer at Fremont High. "Derek knows his older brother from swim team." Technically, that could be true.

Mrs. Sulvana gives me a curt nod. Caro sinks into the car seat. She reaches across the space and gives my hand a quick squeeze.

———

AT SATURDAY'S SPEECH TOURNAMENT, I stagger through the halls. It's Fremont's turn to host, and we're all here early to help set up. The entire team is suffering from some sort of snow and ice hangover. Even Ben is quiet, and Ryan hasn't flirted once all morning.

As for me, my legs ache, like I really was skating with Jeremy all night. My head feels stuffed with cotton balls. Mom even took my temperature before we left the house this morning. But I don't think there's a cure for what I have. I'm not even sure I have anything, just this strange sensation that feels both hollow and heavy. It feels like I've betrayed everyone—Sam, Tory, even Caro. I should feel happy Caro didn't get into trouble; it was a close call. Instead, I feel like I'm coming off a crying jag, or about to head into one.

All morning long, I've checked my cell phone. Now, I pull it out and stare at Sam's number, wondering if I should text him or wait until I see him here. While I'm sorting trophies—at least one of which I'm sure he'll carry home—I decide that this is something you can only explain in person.

Fifteen minutes before the first round, my cell phone buzzes, shaking my skirt pocket. I check it, and my heart starts buzzing as well.

Sam: 42

The biology room seems like an odd choice for practice. I pocket my phone, grab my script, and try not to look like I'm rushing anywhere. I don't want anyone to notice, especially Tory.

Glancing back looks guilty, so I slip from the team room without even a peek over my shoulder.

But I race down the hall and up the stairs, just in case someone followed me. On the landing, I wait, listening, while trying to hush my heart and my breathing. For a full minute, I remain still. When I hear nothing, I start off down the hall.

The door to room 42 is shut, but creaks open when I push on it. Sam is at the back of the room. His hands are folded on the top of his desk, and he's wearing the bland expression of a teacher-judge. Cold light spills from the windows. The space feels strange, too empty, like it's missing Ms. Morgan's nonstop chatter about all things scientific.

"Let's start with F-13," he says, in a perfectly bland teacher-judge kind of way.

But I don't want to pretend this is a tournament round. Not after last night. I want to explain. I want him to understand.

"Sam," I begin.

"Mr. Romero," he says. "Are you participant F-13? If so, please start."

Mr. Romero? Really? So, okay, maybe he wants to practice first, but something sharp squeezes my heart. This isn't anything like Sam. His expression is still too bland, those summer-green eyes almost dull. Without knowing what else to do or say, I walk to the front of the room and read my piece.

"Good," he says when I finish, but the word doesn't sound like praise. He stands and heads for the front of the room. "Scores will be posted outside the main cafeteria doors."

Now I think he's lost his mind, or just taken this role playing thing a little too far. I cut him off before he can step into the hall.

"Sam," I say. "I want ... I want ..." But nothing else comes out of my mouth. All the words I thought I might say vanish. I'm left with nothing except the feel of my teeth against my upper lip.

Donkeys don't talk. At least, this one doesn't. Why, when it's so important, can't I speak up?

"Yeah." Sam jerks open the door. "That's what I thought."

He leaves, but I can't follow. My feet are locked in place. I sway from side to side, but I can't actually move. The cotton balls in my head swirl together until I can't think either. Footsteps pound past the door. There's a rattle, like someone crashed into a locker. The clock on the wall makes one lonely tick.

I glance up at it and see that the first round starts in less than a minute—and I don't know my room number. Now my feet move. I dash down the hall and race for the team room. I spin, my head jerking around, looking for someone, anyone, from Fremont—Tory, Ryan, Mr. Henderson.

Everyone's gone. My heart beats so hard, I think it might get jammed in my ribcage. My chest hurts. What happens if I miss a round? Do I get disqualified? Do I bring down the team score? Do I lose everything? My extra credit, my chance at creative story-telling, all of it, just so Caro could skate with Jeremy?

"Here!" Someone barrels into me. The sharp edge of Tory's heel lands on my foot. Pain shocks tears from my eyes, and I yelp.

"Later." Tory practically growls the word. "We're talking later." She shoves a piece of paper into my hands and then pushes me down the hallway. "Last door on the left," is the only other thing she says to me.

Chapter 11

I HAVE to wait until the first speaker has finished before I can slip into the classroom. The shame of this sets my cheeks on fire. True, I could pretend to be double entered in the tournament and that's what most of the kids in the room are thinking. Except one. Ryan.

He glowers at me, all fierce eyebrows and eyes. I barely have time to register this because the judge in the back of the room calls out:

"F-13. You're up next."

When I stand, she asks, "Have you caught your breath? We can always skip and come back to you."

It's a nice offer, and she looks like a nice judge. I wish I could see her name, but her badge is covered by a scarf looped around her neck. The air around me grows tense. It's like I can feel the other kids bristle. Coming in late is bad enough. I cannot mess with the speaking order on top of it.

I shake my head. "That's okay," I say. "I'll go now."

I give my worst reading ever, worse than the first time I stumbled through *Jane Eyre* in the speech team practice room. But with Ryan glaring at me, all I want to do is hide. My script inches upward, like it used to when Sam started coaching me.

Sam. When I finally sit back down, my lousy performance doesn't bother me nearly as much as the look on Sam's face did. He wasn't angry or disgusted with me, but maybe he should be. No, all I saw in his eyes was disappointment.

Somehow, that's worse.

———

5, 3, 2

My scores make no sense. From the absolute bottom to near the top? In one day? For a long time, I stare at them, getting bumped by other kids checking their own scores. I don't remember being that strong in the last round. Honestly? I don't remember the last round at all.

Before it started, I decided the best way to deal with things was not to be me at all, but Jane. She may be all alone and up on her stool. The superintendent may call her a liar. But she doesn't deserve those things. I'm pretty sure I deserve everything Tory, Ryan, and Sam have thrown at me today. I feel as though I've been up on that stool, battered, bruised, and alone.

I don't go to any final rounds. At first, I hide in a girls' bathroom, and then I find a seat in the auditorium. Bit by bit, kids filter in, but everything is still hushed, the echo of voices soft and comforting. I hear the clip, clip, clip of heels before Tory slips into the row behind me.

She sits so I'd have to swivel around if I want to talk to her. I stay put.

"Thanks for staking out a spot," she says.

I nod.

"I'm going to tell Ryan we need to send an advance party before all the awards ceremonies. Why let Winnetka get the good seats?"

I can't laugh, although I suspect Tory wants me to.

"Okay," she says, "maybe you can help me out. I have something I believe, something I don't believe, and something I can't believe."

That almost has me spinning around, but I stay locked in place.

"Caro and Jeremy Spinner? Yeah, I believe that. What she sees in him is anyone's guess." Tory makes a gagging sound.

I almost do laugh.

"But I believe it. You and Spinner?" She lets this new pairing hang in the air for a moment. "I don't believe that at all. You and Romero?"

My heart slams against my rib cage so hard, I think it bruises something inside me. I hold my breath and wait for what Tory will say next.

"That's something I can't believe ... but maybe I should?"

This last is a question. She wants an answer. I should give her one. But explaining? Where do I start? Do I give up Caro's secrets? Do I give up Sam's? Do I give up mine? I shut my eyes, press a hand against my mouth, and wish that the whole world would go away.

More kids fill the rows in front and behind us. The Winnetka girls sashay in, but slow down when they reach Tory and me. Annika opens her mouth, but Tory points a finger at her and then at the floor—a classic *you're going down* gesture. They scurry into a row several feet away, and Tory laughs.

"I kicked her butt in the extemporaneous speaking final and she knows it." Tory sounds triumphant, but it doesn't last. "So, anything I should know?"

I shake my head. It isn't lying if I don't say anything.

———

MONDAY MORNING AT SCHOOL, I haven't even made it to my locker when Caro grabs me and then Jeremy and drags us into an empty classroom. The door closes with a click that matches the determination on Caro's face.

"You two need to pretend to go together this week," Caro says.

Jeremy and I inch our gazes toward each other. I'm sure I look as repulsed by this idea as he does.

"Babe," Jeremy begins.

"Don't 'babe' me." Caro sticks a finger in his face. She's fierce. For an instant I see Mrs. Sulvana in her features. "My mom is going to be here all freaking week long, if you can believe that." Caro exhales. "God, I wish she would stop with all the volunteering. She'll be helping in the office and running the PIE meeting."

Well, Mrs. Sulvana does love PIE. But the Parent Information Exchange always meets in the middle of the school day, which means we're not going to be able to escape Caro's mom.

"I told her that you and Jolia are going together. So you need to act like you really are."

Jeremy's jaw is slack. I shake my head.

"I *had* to," Caro says. "She kept asking about it, so I finally made up a story that you two are going together. But your parents." Caro points at me, "Don't know, and you're afraid to tell them."

That's not a made-up story. That's real life with the starring role recast. *Now playing the part of the beautiful Caro is plain understudy Jolia.*

"It's just for this week," she says. "While my mom is here. Then you guys can "break up" and everything will go back to normal." Caro draws little air quotes around "break up." She should probably put them around "going together" as well, since there's no way anyone in this school will believe Jeremy Spinner is going out with me. Didn't Tory make that clear on Saturday?

"A week," Jeremy says like it's detention.

"It's that, or nothing. She's already suspicious. If she finds out, I'll probably be grounded for life. A week, and I promise, things will go back to normal."

I sigh. Like sneaking around is normal? There's another word that needs air quotes. What happens the next time Caro's mom gets suspicious? Will I have to pretend to go with Jeremy until we graduate?

"No one is going to believe this," I say. "Everyone in school knows you guys are going together."

"Only my mom needs to believe."

Jeremy and I exchange another glance. Okay, so we don't like each other. But we both would do anything for Caro. Even this. I hold out my hand and Jeremy shakes it.

"Not like that," Caro says. She pulls our right hands apart, then slips my right into Jeremy's left. "Like this. You're going together, remember?"

It's going to be hard to forget.

———

AT LUNCH, Caro meets me at the cafeteria door, an arm thrown out so I can't walk in.

"My mom's in there." She rolls her eyes. "She volunteered for lunch monitor duty."

"I'm still hungry," I say. Actually, I'm starving. I barely ate all day Sunday, thoughts of Sam chasing away my appetite. Today, I'd gladly inhale the healthy-for-you flatbread and tomato paste they try to convince us is real pizza.

"You won't be when I tell you." Caro looks at the floor. "Mymomthinksyou'reabadinfluence."

"What?" Her mumbled words don't make any sense, but they sound bad.

"My mom," Caro tries again. "After I told her all that stuff about you and Jeremy going together, she decided you're a bad influence on me. She doesn't want us to hang out."

The pit of my stomach ices over. I know I'm not actually losing Caro, but it feels like it. "You do realize that you're actually a bad influence on yourself? Or me, for that matter?"

"Yes, yes, I know," she snaps. "It's just for a week."

"Really? I'll still be a bad influence, even if I "break up" with Jeremy, right?" I draw the little quotes in the air. I'm beginning to think you could fit my entire life inside them.

"She'll forget about it the next time you help me with my math homework." Caro shrugs, and it's like that's what all this is to her: one big shoulder shrug. "And it's not like you're *really* going with anyone."

She doesn't say it to be mean. Even so, the words sting.

"So what you're saying is—"

"You need to eat lunch somewhere else," she finishes. "All week."

"All week," I echo.

Caro shoves a sack lunch into my hands. "Please? Go on. I brought money."

With that, Caro vanishes into the cafeteria. I stand there as if the ice in my stomach has spread to each limb. My fingers crumple the brown paper sack, but that's it. That's all I can move.

Bit by bit, I melt. I roll my shoulders, loosening them up. But I freeze again when Mrs. Sulvana bustles past the cafeteria door. Normally, she'd say hello. Normally, she'd stop and talk to me about school or my grades or whatever. Not today. Today, she's all stern, her eyes dark and cold. She doesn't say a word.

Once she's gone, I glance at the sack lunch in my hands and wonder if she recognized it. I wonder if that even matters. I turn, not sure where to eat lunch—a stairwell, a dark classroom, maybe the girls' bathroom, no matter how gross that is.

That's when I see Ryan Dinsmore. He's leaning against a locker, and it looks like he's been there for a while. If you could take curiosity and wrap it all up in pity, it would match the expression on his face. I wonder how much he's heard. I wonder how much he knows.

I wonder how much he's going to tell Tory.

———

HOLDING hands with Jeremy is like being a puppy dragged along by a leash. I think—then try not to think—about holding hands with Sam and how different that felt.

For Caro's sake, I pretend. So does Jeremy. We have no choice. Mrs. Sulvana is everywhere at school. Still, as the days go on, I get better at being his girlfriend. It's like acting—or pretending. Right now, it's good to pretend to be someone else, a different girl, the sort who'd go out with Jeremy Spinner. This girl isn't failing speech, isn't lying to the whole school. Her heart doesn't ache every time she thinks of a boy named Sam. Even though there is nothing real about it, being Jeremy's girlfriend is easy.

Amazingly, Jeremy and I discover we have something in common besides Caro and laser tag. We both like science, even though he's failing biology in a dramatic fashion. For lunch we head up to the Biology classroom. Ms. Morgan has all sorts of activities for extra credit, which I don't need, but Jeremy does.

And even though it's room 42, and even though I think of Sam every single time I walk through the door, the space feels different during the school week.

I talk Jeremy through online dissections. At first, his enthusiasm disturbs me. Then I realize it's more for *online* than *dissection*.

"Don't tell anyone," he says. "But when Ms. Morgan brought in the fetal pigs, I had to run for the bathroom. I ... I—" He shakes his head. "I can't do it."

"You could've told me," comes Ms. Morgan's soft reprimand from the back of the room.

Jeremy's shoulders sag.

"I won't tell," I say. "Not even Caro."

He jerks up and stares at me, a look of disbelief on his face. I cross my heart, then pretend to lock my lips with a key.

Now he looks at me like I'm a dork, which means things are back to normal.

All week long, girls give me funny looks. No one talks to me unless it's to say: "How's Jeremy today?" But there's nothing nice in the way anyone asks this.

Most girls don't say a word; they just scoot their chair away from mine. In every class there's a huge space between my desk and everyone else's. Whispered words prick my ears. I doubt they're very nice words, but I don't ask anyone to repeat them. Maybe I should. Maybe I should demand to know what's going on, why people keep talking about me. But I can't find the words, and so instead, I swallow all my questions until it feels like they might choke me.

Speech team practice has been weird all week, but not as awful as everything else. Kaitlin and Savannah talk to me—sort of. Ryan just smirks, a strange smile that I work overtime to ignore. Tory is oddly quiet. Still, compared to the rest of the school day, practice feels like a refuge. In this room, I'm not Jolia, Jeremy Spinner's pretend girlfriend. I can be Jane on her stool. I find that role the most comforting of all.

At last Friday arrives with its weekly ritual of gathering around Ryan's laptop and refreshing the Winnetka Speech Team site until they update their roster. I reach the room five minutes late. Everyone's huddled around a single desk. Ryan's sprawled out again, of course, so all I can see of him are the soles of his sneakers.

"He's not there!" Ryan cries out. A second later, his shoes vanish and his feet thud against the floor.

"What?" Tory says.

"Romero. He's not on the roster. No great speeches, no discussion. Nothing."

"No way. Let me see." Tory pushes her way through the crowd and takes Ryan's laptop from him.

"Hey!" he says, but she sets the computer down on an empty desk.

"What do you think it is?" Savannah asks.

"We need to do some investigating," Tory says. "Find out if he was in school today. This isn't the official tournament roster."

Ryan groans. "If he shows up in discussion, I'm throwing myself out a window."

My stomach jumps, and my heart flutters. I feel sick, and wonder if Sam really is. Or if his name missing from the roster has something to do with me.

"Someone," Tory says, "could find out." She raises her eyes so they meet mine. "Someone. Could." Each word is slow, deliberate, and meant just for me.

I could. Maybe. I could pull out my phone and send him a text. After last week, I don't know if he'll answer. After last week, I don't have the courage to text him at all.

I give my head the slightest of shakes. "I can't," I mouth.

Tory raises an eyebrow. "Really?"

"Really," I say, this time, my voice loud.

A few girls glance at me, but I can tell no one thinks much of it. For all they know, I'm still going with Jeremy and haven't even spoken to Sam.

Tory refreshes the page again, her eyes narrowed to tiny slits as she scans the screen. "Wait a second," she says. "They just updated the doc. He will be there, doing great speeches and ..." Tory pauses, her face filled with mischief.

Ryan sits up. "And?"

"Discussion!"

He slumps in his chair as if he's suddenly lost all his bones.

"You were saying something about a window?" Tory adds.

Something flutters inside me—it feels like the excitement before Christmas morning—or the feeling you get right before you see the dentist. But I keep my face bland. I don't move an inch. Because Tory? She's staring at me hard.

It's only later, out in the lobby, that Tory says something to me. I'm waiting for the last activity bus. Her book bag whispers against her wool coat. It's such a soft sound, nothing like Tory herself. For several moments, she stands next to me, still oddly quiet. At last, she speaks.

"Rumor has it you stole Jeremy from Caro."

"I did what...?" I trail off and stare at the ceiling. This is just my luck. All those words, whispered behind my back? Now I understand every last one, and I really wish I didn't.

"Not that I believe it," she adds. "It's clear you can't stand him, and vice versa."

"It's clear," I say, "or did you hear that from Ryan?"

"Maybe a little of both." She grins, but I don't feel like smiling back. "Look," she continues. "I don't know what's going on. But if you feel like talking ... or giving up the goods on Romero."

I can't help it. I snort. Tory, always scheming about something.

She laughs. "Doesn't hurt to ask. Really, if you feel like talking?" She shrugs. "Believe it or not, I do know how to listen. My cell and email are on the team roster."

Outside, a car horn honks. Tory hefts her messenger bag. When she reaches the door, she turns, waves, and then vanishes into early evening flurries. The door whooshes closed, my own wave coming too late. A moment later, a loud clomping fills the hallway. Ryan skids into the lobby, hops on one foot, then charges through the double doors. A second later, they fly back open.

"Hey, Cuppernull," he says. "For the record, I don't believe it either."

Really? I think. Out loud, I say, "Wow. I didn't know you could move that fast."

He makes a face, but beneath the frown is an actual smile, not a smirk. Then he, too, is gone.

Chapter 12

SATURDAY'S SNOW flurries don't keep us from traveling to St. Peter for the speech tournament. I sit behind Kaitlin and Savannah, but everything feels like ice—the bus seats, the floor, their stares. Before the first round starts, I check my phone, then check it again, and check it so many times, I'm afraid I'll drain the battery. Casually, I walk by the Winnetka girls, hoping to hear where Sam is.

I get nothing but a whispered, *"You're going down."*

In the break before the third round, I see him. Sam. He's here. For the first time in days, relief fills me. Finally, something—or someone—that's right. We'll talk, and somehow everything will be okay.

Only when he's closer do I notice how tight his face is. How he's looking straight at me, but I don't think he really sees me. He walks past without saying a word, without nodding his head. Nothing. It comes like a blow, fast and hard to my stomach. I'm trying very hard to take a full breath while fighting back tears.

Then the cell phone in my skirt pocket vibrates.

Sam: 24

I dash down the hall, taking the same route Sam did. I round a corner and find Room 24, a chemistry lab. Inside, the lights are off, and gray daylight filters in from a few windows. It's dreary, and a harsh smell makes my nose wrinkle. I can't identify the odor, but I'm pretty sure it's the scent of failure.

"I thought we'd try something different today." Sam hands me a script.

I take it, totally uncertain about what's going on. His brows are drawn together, his jaw all tense. I glance at the script. It's Shakespeare, but *Hamlet* this time. In the middle of the page, one line is highlighted in yellow.

This above all: to thine own self be true.

I don't know what it means, at least not what it means about us —or me.

"Everyone says you're going together." Sam beats his script against his leg and the pages flutter. "You and Jeremy Spinner."

I don't nod. I don't shake my head. I stand there, the first traces of donkey teeth making themselves known beneath my upper lip. Only then do I realize that I've hardly felt them all day—until now.

"Everyone?" I say at last.

"Girls on your team," he adds, "girls on mine. They all seemed really happy to tell me about it."

I bet they were. It was crazy, but I didn't like the idea of Sam talking to all those other girls. "It isn't something that's true," I say.

"Yeah. I know."

He does? He understands? I can explain without betraying Caro. I don't have the words, not yet, but I will. I'm positive. I'm about to take a step forward and—I don't know—maybe hug him.

He holds up a hand. "That's not the problem."

Wait. There's still a problem?

"I think you're pretending. And the problem with that is I think you might be pretending about a lot of things."

A lot of things? Or just us?

"I can explain," I say, but at the same time, my mind whirls. How? How am I going to explain? I'm standing at the crossroads of the same exact decision: Caro or Sam? Sam or Caro? Who do I pick? And why can't I pick both?

By the time I make up my mind, it's too late. Sam spins away and heads for the door.

"You need to figure out what parts of you are true." He pauses, his hand on the doorknob. "And I can't help you with that."

The door clicks shut behind him. I stand, surrounded by the stench of failure, and push the tears from my cheeks.

———

"WHAT'S up with your third round?" Tory flops into the bus seat in front of mine and rests her chin on its edge.

Since I never checked my scores, I have no idea what she's talking about. Why check? No way I made the finals. And texting them to Sam? That's something I don't get to do anymore. I shake my head, hoping that works as an answer.

"Two, two, and a five." She counts the scores off on her fingers. "Did you crash and burn during your last round?"

Yes, I think. That's it exactly.

"It happens," she says, "especially when you start getting better. You know, one step forward and two back." She shrugs. "That sort of thing. With a little more stamina, you'll end up making the final round."

This time, when I shake my head, I mean it. "That's not happening," I say.

"Maybe not until next season." Tory sing-songs the words, so I'm not sure if she's teasing me or not. "But don't count yourself out for this one, not yet."

Does she really believe I can make the finals *this* year? I don't believe it, and when you get right down to it, that's the only part that matters.

"So, this thing with you and Jeremy Spinner—"

I sigh. "It's not what you think it is," I say, wishing I had at least said that much to Sam.

"I think I have a pretty good idea."

Yes, I'm sure she does.

She leans her head back against the window and adds, "What about this thing with you and Sam Romero?"

I squeeze my eyes shut. "There is no thing with me and Sam Romero."

At last. I've finally told the truth about something.

———

BEFORE FIRST BELL on Monday morning, Jeremy finds me. He drags me to the biology classroom. Under the cover of online squid dissection, he starts talking, fast.

"Why don't we pretend to cool it," he says. "I'll act like I'm avoiding you cuz I want to break up but don't want to hurt your feelings."

He's given this a lot of thought. I'm almost impressed. Almost. "Why do you get to dump me?"

He raises his hands, indicating the whole package that is Jeremy Spinner. Oh, of course. No girl would *ever* dump him. Please. I look away and roll my eyes. But I don't really care—that much. After last week, getting dumped by him might be the best thing that's ever happened to me.

I don't see Caro all day. Not in the halls. Not at lunch. Her spot in the cafeteria goes empty while Jeremy has rejoined the jocks. I retreat to room 42, where it seems like this whole mess started. I do a virtual heart dissection for extra credit—not that I need it—and wonder how easy it is to break something that looks so strong.

Still, I'm pretty sure Caro is in school. I'm hoping to catch her after last bell and before speech team practice. Like last week, she finds me—and Jeremy—first. Again, she drags us into an empty classroom. She shuts the door behind us, then leans against it as if we'll try to escape. The anger in her eyes makes me think we might want to do that.

"What is going on?" she says.

"We're cooling things off." With immense pride, Jeremy points between me and him. "So we can "break up" tomorrow." He draws those air quotes and gives Caro a grin.

I nod. "Jeremy actually had a good idea."

He shoots me a look. Only then do I realize how bad that sounds.

Caro speaks like she hasn't even heard us. "You know how many rumors there are about you guys?"

I shake my head. Jeremy does the same. But he drops his gaze to the floor, and I know we're both lying. And how fair is it that the rumors make him look like a stud and me like the last person anyone wants to be around?

"Well, guess what everyone is saying," Caro adds. "That you two go up to the biology room, and—"

"Do schoolwork?" I say.

"Jolia helped me with all the make-up dissections," Jeremy says. "I'm getting a B." He makes this sound like he's discovered a new species.

"Make up or make *out?*" Caro's words and her eyes burn into us.

"Caro," I begin, "don't be crazy."

"It's what everyone is talking about." She waves her hands as if the whole school is in this room.

Jeremy and I look stupid for pretending we hadn't heard.

"But I don't really believe it," she says.

I sag with relief.

"You know what I do believe? I think you two." She points to me, then Jeremy, her finger stabbing the air. "Want the rumors to be true."

I look at Jeremy, and he looks at me. Maybe, in that moment, we should've both looked at Caro. She can't see the disbelief on our faces—the revulsion, if you want to get precise. She can't see how we've been counting the seconds until our "break up."

"See?" Her voice is pitched high, almost a shriek. "It's true. You've been avoiding me all week."

"Oh, my god, really? You told us to!" I gesture at Jeremy. He needs to do or say something—anything—a "Hey, babe," or somehow pull out a magical bouquet of grocery store flowers.

But his mouth hangs open, arms slack at his side. It's like Caro's words have turned him into a zombie. I want to shake him—hard.

"Why didn't you text or call this weekend?" Caro says.

Why didn't I? Besides being completely wrecked over Sam? "Your mom? Remember? I'm a 'bad influence'." And yeah, I use the air quotes.

Caro rolls her eyes. I think that's what does it.

"Oh, so it's all about you?" I say. "Never mind the whole school thinks I'm a boyfriend-stealing skank, this whole thing has totally screwed up any chance I had with a guy from Winnetka—"

"Sam Romero?" Jeremy says this.

Caro and I both startle at his voice.

"Yeah." My voice goes soft, the words hard to say. "Sam."

"Why don't I know about this guy?" Caro asks.

This time, Jeremy actually rolls his eyes. How he knows about

Sam, I'm not sure, but clearly his observation skills are better than Caro's.

"Because we never talk, unless it's about Jeremy," I tell her, "so I figured why bother even saying anything." This is a half-truth. True, she's been all about Jeremy lately, but then I haven't offered up any information about me—not about Sam, or failing speech, or anything. Still, I see that my words cut.

"Well, I guess now that won't be a problem for you."

Caro flings open the door. It crashes against the jamb and the air shakes.

"Come on, babe," Jeremy says. "Don't be stupid." A second later, his eyes go wide in horror. Even he knows this was the wrong thing to say.

"What did you call me?" Caro's fingers grip the door so hard, they go white.

"I didn't mean it like that. I only—"

"So there's a *good* way to be stupid? Well, guess what? You won't have to worry about that anymore. We're through!"

She runs, but I can't force my legs to follow her. My legs don't want to follow her. My legs are done with that. All I can do is sink into a chair, plant my arms on the desk, and rest my head in them. I try to calculate what I've lost in the last week—my reputation, my best friend, my maybe boyfriend. No matter how I do the math, I can't seem to add up how it all happened.

"What was that?" Jeremy says.

"I think Caro just broke up with us," I say.

He swears and flops down next to me. "This makes no sense. She *wanted* us to pretend."

"I know."

I need to get to speech practice. Jeremy, I think, starts track today. But we sit there, like we're both broken inside. If I try to walk, I think my legs might crumble beneath me. Somehow, I do stand, and Jeremy follows. We stumble to the door, then part. He heads for the locker rooms. I find the nearest stairwell but turn before climbing the stairs.

Jeremy walks away, completely drained of his jock swagger. He looks like he's missing a piece of something important. When he turns and stares at me, I know that he is. And that I am, too.

————

BY TUESDAY LUNCH, I feel like I'm in deep freeze with Caro. I thought once she cooled off, once it was clear Jeremy and I truly have "broken up," we could talk this through. Nothing works. Not phoning, not texting, not even a handwritten note shoved through the vents of her locker. What happens now? What happens to our graphic novel, our retelling of *Romeo and Juliet*? What happens to *us*? I plan to talk to her at lunch, but when I reach the cafeteria, Jeremy's blocking the doorway.

"You don't want to go in there," he says.

"What?"

"Trust me, Jolia."

My name stops me. I think it's the first time he's ever said it *to* me, not just about me. "What's going on?" I ask.

He scoots to let a few freshmen squeeze past and I peer in. Caro isn't at our usual table, the one next to all of Jeremy's friends. At first, I don't see her. I let my gaze bounce from table to table, taking in each group, cataloging them quickly: gymnasts, swimmers, speech team.

Speech team. As a backup, I'd been thinking of sitting there today, but now I can't.

Caro's sitting there.

"Why is Caro at the speech table?" I ask Jeremy.

"I figured that's where you'd sit today." He shrugs. "I know she can be kind of—" He stares into the cafeteria as if they're serving the words he needs along with the main entrée. "Well, kind of bitchy. But she's not mean like that. She wouldn't steal your other ... friends."

Well, not unless she thinks I stole Jeremy. But the Caro I know —or at least thought I knew—wouldn't. But I'm not sure I know anyone anymore, especially myself.

He holds up a vinyl lunch sack. "I brought mine today." He doesn't say, *just in case*, but I hear it in his tone.

We walk toward the stairs as if we're headed for the biology classroom, but we don't make it there. We sit on the steps halfway up, hidden from everyone. Jeremy opens the sack, pulls out a sandwich, and offers me half.

"You don't mind?" I say.

"I've got two more, and it's not like you eat a lot."

Maybe not in Jeremy terms.

The stairwell is quiet, and I'm afraid I'm chewing much too loudly. I can hear the lettuce from the sandwich crackle in my ears with each bite. This is weird, and a little freaky, and the donkey teeth want to make a grand reappearance. With my tongue, I touch my front two teeth, and the sensation melts away. It's a small comfort today.

"This sucks," Jeremy says after his second sandwich.

It does. It really does.

"I tried all last night," he continues, his voice tense, like he's a can of soda about to burst. "I emailed and called. I even went over to her house and did that thing guys do in the movies. You know, toss pebbles at a window."

Visions of glass shattered all over Caro's bedroom fill my mind. "What happened?"

"Their crazy dog started barking, so I ran away." He heaves a sigh. "Sometimes there's no talking to her. I mean, I can say stuff to you and not worry about pissing you off."

"You do piss me off," I say. "You just don't care if you do."

"I do," he insists, but I'm not sure I believe him. "It's just different with Caro."

"That's because I don't matter, and Caro does."

"You matter," he says.

"Just not to you."

Just when I think he won't respond, he speaks again.

"Does Sam Romero matter?"

Something pings inside me like Jeremy's words have set off a firecracker. My throat is all tight, and I have that shaken-up can of soda feeling in my chest.

"No," I say at last.

"I think you're lying."

"He doesn't want to talk to me," I say, "not after the winter carnival."

"You know, it sounds crazy, but I'm thinking that it might've been better if Caro's mom had caught us." He stares into the depths of his lunch sack as if all the answers we need are in there. "At least that would've been honest."

I think that's the smartest thing Jeremy Spinner has ever said.

Chapter 13

ALL WEEK LONG, I eat lunch with Jeremy in the stairwell. Caro spends every lunch hour at the speech team table, and every afternoon, everyone at speech team practice acts like this is no big deal. The only difference is Tory points her digital camera my way with a fierceness I haven't seen all season. She's convinced I can make the final round, maybe even this Saturday at the Big 9 tournament.

"Can I ask you a favor?" I say on Thursday afternoon. I've run through my piece at least five times. I know it by heart, and only glance at my script because if you hold one in a round, you need to at least appear to refer to it. But I feel safer just hanging onto it. Sam's words echo in my head: *Not a prop or a crutch.* I've seen some kids perform without a script at all. I'll never be that brave, so I think yes, it's a crutch.

"Turn the camera off?" Tory grins at me.

"Actually, I'm giving my last speech in Mr. Henderson's class tomorrow." I swallow hard. "Would you film it? You know, for practice?"

An odd look crosses her face. "Okay," she says, "sure."

The last speech is a how-to speech, and it's thirty percent of our grade. This one speech is the difference between passing and failing. Even with the extra credit from the speech team, I still need every percentage point I can get. We duck into the empty world languages room, and Tory sets up the camera while I get everything ready.

"What's the topic?" she asks.

I hold back the smile. "How to overcome the fear of public speaking."

A single heartbeat passes, then Tory bursts out laughing. She laughs for so long, I suspect she's laughing *at* me, not *with* me.

"Sorry, sorry," she says, and wipes her eyes. "It's just ... it's just ..." She gulps a breath. "It's just so perfect."

"It's got to be," I mutter.

I go through my speech, pulling in everything I've learned from Tory, from Sam, and a few things I've invented on my own. Like how you don't have to look anyone directly in the eye as long as you can fake it. Stare at a spot over their shoulder—or their uni-brow.

Tory snorts at this.

"Should I cut uni-brow?" I ask.

"Are you kidding? Henderson loves that sort of thing."

She smiles when I mention the pencil trick and speaking into the mirror. I end my speech with advice on finding what you love about the topic, as motivation to speak up.

"It's pretty good," Tory says when I finish.

From where I stand, *pretty good* must be better than *not bad*.

"Want to watch it?" she asks.

Not really. My teeth behaved while I spoke, but I feel them now, just a hint. But since I asked Tory to film me, not watching the video would be stupid. So I nod and suck in a deep breath. I weave my fingers together and hold on tight so I won't give into the urge to hide behind my hands.

Tory presses Play. I survive. Maybe tomorrow won't be as bad as I think.

———

THE FINAL SPEECH evaluation is the only one Mr. Henderson doesn't hand back right away. We'll find out how we did once grades for the third term go in. After class, a few kids come up to me, asking about the pencil trick.

"Try it," I say. "It sounds kind of crazy, but it works."

Another girl asks if practicing in front of her doll collection would help. I think of the tournament rounds, all sorts of eyes on me, beady and small. I nod. A doll collection would be perfect.

At lunch, I bypass the cafeteria automatically, my gaze straight ahead. I clutch my brown bag and head for the stairwell. Every day, I tell myself this will be the day Jeremy rejoins his friends. So far, he hasn't.

Today is no exception. He's here, with a massive lunch. I sit on the same step, but there's plenty of air between us.

"Hey," he says, "I've been talking to some of my bros."

Really? *Bros?* Ugh.

"About you being a skank."

"What?"

He holds up a hand, one clutching a sandwich, but it's enough to stop me. "I mean, not one. I told them you were tutoring me in biology, but I made up a story we were going out because I was embarrassed to be failing."

A strange sort of pang hits me. Something about making up a story and being embarrassed about failing—who knew Jeremy Spinner and I had something else in common?

"They believed you?" I ask.

"Oh, come on," he says. "You're on the speech team, in knitting club, and orchestra." He draws out this last word so, in my head, I hear *leprosy*. "Besides, I'm getting a B, so of course they believed me. In fact, some of them might ask for your help."

"There was this guy at my locker this morning," I say. "Lukas, I think."

"Yeah." Jeremy taps his forehead. "He's not that bright."

This, from Jeremy Spinner, is a condemnation. Or irony. Or both.

"I thought he was a creeper."

"He's okay, but he's probably failing something."

After a moment, I say, "Thanks." I'm kind of surprised I mean it, too.

"It's probably the least I can do, what with everything." He raises a hand and lets it fall as if this everything is too heavy for even him to lift.

Five minutes before the bell rings, Jeremy asks about the Big 9 speech tournament.

"It's the big one before sub-sectionals," I tell him. "Tory says it's when the teams start gunning for state—there are lots of upsets and surprises."

"What about Romero?" he asks.

"What about him?" I cringe because the words come out sharper than I mean them to.

"We share the indoor field with Winnetka," he says. "And I heard a few things."

"What did you hear?" My insides revolt. The carrot sticks I'm eating form a lump in my stomach. I think I might throw up.

Jeremy shakes his head. "Nothing that makes sense, at least, not to me. Something about a ring."

"A ring for what?"

"See, that's what I don't get, but the Winnetka guys were talking about it." Jeremy pauses and considers the stack of Oreos resting in his palm. He—very generously—offers me one. "But it wasn't really about Romero."

I sense more than see him turn his head. He stares straight on, and I feel his gaze against my cheek.

"It was about you."

———

I'M DASHING down the hall, late for speech practice, when Mrs. Riley, the creative storytelling teacher, catches me.

"Jolia, walk."

Yes, we're supposed to walk in school, not that it's stopped anyone from running. Jeremy and his friends race up and down the corridors, and no one ever stops them. But I slow down and do a funny race-walk thing.

Mrs. Riley laughs and falls into step next to me. "Are you looking forward to creative storytelling?"

I nod because she expects no less. At the moment, I don't know if I'll be sitting in her classroom on Monday morning. This is also something I don't feel like explaining.

"Have you and Caro started working on your project already?"

"Sort of," I say, which is as close to the truth as I can get. For once, failing speech looks like the better option. How did that happen? And how, on Monday, will I ever work with Caro if we're not even speaking to each other?

Mrs. Riley halts in a teacher sort of way that means I must stop walking too. "Jolia, are you okay?"

I nod, but that's a lie. My throat is tight, but finally, I squeak out, "I'm late for speech practice."

Mrs. Riley smiles at me, then does the weirdest thing. She turns her back on me, then gives me a little wave, the sort that means, *hurry, hurry, hurry*.

"I never saw you," she says, and I can hear the laughter in her voice.

I rush down the hall.

I'm almost to the speech team room when I see two people who are not where they're supposed to be. Jeremy should be at track practice. Caro should be in her mom's car on the way home. Neither of them should be huddled in an empty classroom. From where I stand, I can't tell if their whispers are happy or fierce, if it's a fight—or if they're making up. Their faces are close enough for kissing—or spitting. It's like watching a couple in a movie, only I have no idea how this story will end.

A hand—I think it's Jeremy's—shuts the door. With that one simple act, he's closed off everything. This is what I've been afraid of all year, from the second they started going together. I've lost Caro. She's been gone long before she dumped me on Monday.

My heart thuds heavy and slow in my chest. I stare at that closed door, but the movie is over, or at least, my part in it is. I raise my hand in a goodbye wave. Then I continue down the hall.

———————

"I'M TELLING YOU, he's not on the list."

In the speech team room, Tory and Ryan are playing tug of war with his laptop—a sure sign it's a Friday before a tournament.

"And I'm reminding you," she says, "that you said the same thing last week. What if they know we're hitting the site and are just messing with us?"

"Does it matter?" I ask.

Both Ryan and Tory freeze, like we've pressed pause on one of Tory's endless videos of us. Actually, everyone in the room goes quiet.

"Well." Tory clears her throat. "Of course it matters."

"How?"

"It's just that ... we like to be prepared is all."

"Does Henderson know you do this?" I can't believe this is the first time I've thought to ask. "Technically, aren't you hacking?"

"Legacy," Ryan says, as if that explains everything.

"Huh?" This is Ben, and I'm grateful he's always around to ask the dumb question in the most direct way possible.

"Last year's co-captains gave us Winnetka's login info. It's not our fault they haven't changed the password." Ryan puts his feet up on a chair, but I'm not sure he's as confident as he looks.

This sounds shaky. "Are you sure you should? It's not like we're going to change anything." I point at Ryan. "Either Romero will be in discussion and ruin your life—or he won't. Either he'll give a great speech—or he won't."

"Mentally prepared," Tory says, her voice stronger now. She lets go of the laptop, and Ryan hugs it to his chest. "It's not all here." She taps a script lying on a desk. "A lot of it is up here." She taps her head. "So, if we know where Romero is slotted this week." She shrugs. "It helps."

Does it really? Which would be worse, I wonder. Seeing Caro and Jeremy together today or finding out Monday at lunch? I picture myself, alone in the stairwell, waiting for Jeremy, or peering into the cafeteria, Caro back in her old spot, me totally alone. Maybe Tory has a point. Mentally prepared. But my heart? I'm not sure you can prepare that.

I hold out my hand and, to my surprise, Ryan passes me the laptop without a word. I don't refresh the page. Instead, I click back to the main page, the one with the team picture. Strange as it sounds, I can feel the eyes of the Winnetka girls on me, like they're about to taunt, *"You're going down."*

But it's Sam I stare at.

I barely notice when Tory slips into the desk next to mine.

"Don't suppose you're ready to give up the goods," she says, voice low.

"There's nothing to give." Not anymore, at least. "But—"

Tory leans forward. "Yes?"

The anticipation on her face makes me laugh. "Jeremy said

something today about the Winnetka guys on the team, talking about me."

She slumps in her chair. "Trust me, you don't want those kinds of details."

"No, it was weird. They kept talking about a ring."

Tory tugs me by the shirt sleeve, and we head into the hallway.

"Word for word, what did he say."

So I repeat what I remember from lunch.

Tory shakes her head in disgust. "That makes no sense."

"It's secondhand from Jeremy Spinner," I say. "Did you expect it to?"

Tory sighs. "I need to do some investigating tonight."

"You're like Sherlock Holmes," I say.

"Yeah, well, at least he had Dr. Watson."

"What about Ryan?"

"Watson was a friend." She leaves me standing in the hallway and heads back to the classroom. In a moment, she and Ryan are playing tug-of-war with the laptop again.

A friend. Of all the things Tory has, I wonder if this is the one thing she doesn't.

Chapter 14

BEST BLACK SKIRT. New gray top. I add the blue-gray scarf I finished knitting last night. Since I'm Jane Eyre at boarding school, I don't want to dress too flashy. Vanilla chai deodorant.

Okay, so they didn't have Starbucks in Victorian England.

Clouds cover the sky as the bus pulls from Fremont High. We travel south toward Mankato East High School, and the sun makes its appearance, just a small sliver at first. When we arrive, it's to a sunburst of warmth. Tory steps from the bus, tips her head toward the sky, and smiles.

"It's a good omen," she says.

Ryan comes up behind her, pats her arm. "It is."

Today, they are a united front. They're here to win. I tip my face upward as well. I let the sun warm my skin and inhale air that's trying hard to smell like spring. The second I'm inside the school, I miss the sunshine. Near the entrance is a large open area with tables and chairs. I can't tell if this area is for eating or studying or what, but it's where we stash our coats.

Kids from other teams mill around. Some wander off to find a classroom to practice in. Others gather at the water fountain, so if you actually want a drink, you have to fight your way in. My fingers touch the cell phone in my pocket. It hasn't vibrated, and I know it won't. And although I've seen plenty of Winnetka kids so far, I haven't caught sight of Sam.

I'm not sure what I'd say if I did see him.

I'm thinking of practicing on my own when Tory comes up behind me. She grabs my elbow hard and tugs me away from the collection of tables in the common area.

"Ow," I say. "What are you doing?"

"Come on," she says.

I reach for my script.

"Leave it."

"But—"

"This is ... this is... well, you won't believe it."

Her voice is so stressed and urgent, I follow. When she starts to run for a classroom at the end of a long hall, I race after her.

"Shut the door," she says to me. She's gasping, but still has that star speaker quality, and I do what she says. She shakes her phone. "Work, work. I've got a signal. *Work.*"

Then I hear another voice, coming from the phone's speaker.

"Tory, you there?"

It's Caro.

I push a lump down my throat. I don't know what's going on, but Caro face-timing on Tory's phone can't be anything good.

"Okay, got you," Tory says. "Jolia, come here. This is kind of complicated."

"I thought that was a Facebook status."

Tory eyes me, hard, so I inch forward until I can see the screen. Caro looks like she's inside a strange, sparkly cave. Then I recognize her skirts and tops and realize she's hiding in her closet. From the phone's speaker come the muffled grunts of her little sisters fighting outside the door.

"I have maybe five minutes." Caro sounds angry.

"Same here," Tory says. "Just tell Jolia what Jeremy told you."

My mind flashes to yesterday—Caro, Jeremy, and a closed classroom door. I open my mouth to say something, but Tory shoots me a look so sharp, it kills all my words.

"He thought it was weird that the Winnetka guys were talking about you so much," Caro begins, "so after lunch on Friday, he did some texting."

Really? I'm a little amazed by this.

"They kept calling you a ringer and mentioning the speech team," Caro continues. "He showed me all the messages because he thought it was some special speech team thing."

Ring? Ringer? I try to connect this with what Jeremy told me at lunch. Like then, it still makes no sense. It's certainly not a speech team thing. I frown, then peer at Tory. She holds up her free hand and nods at Caro.

"He asked me about it, since I'd been sitting at the speech team table—" Caro pauses and cringes, I think, but the screen is so dark, I can't tell.

"So I asked Tory about it," Caro finishes.

"So I did a little snooping last night. Today Ryan and I cornered a Winnetka girl. It's funny." She pauses, her forehead scrunched like she's puzzled. "She was really happy to tell us. It's almost like they wanted us to find out. You want to know what they think?"

This isn't a question that needs an answer. It's clear Tory can't wait to tell me.

"They think you're a ringer!" she declares.

Hadn't we established none of us knows what that means? I shake my head, showing her I'm clueless.

"You're a plant," Tory explains.

"With leaves?" Okay, so it's a classic Ben sort of question, but I still have no idea what she means.

Caro snorts. Tory sighs and rolls her eyes.

146

"They think you've been purposely performing badly at tournaments so Winnetka will be lulled into placing a less talented speaker into the prose category." Tory speaks slowly like I'm all of three years old. "Then today or at sub-sectionals, you're supposed to blow everyone out of the water."

This is the craziest thing I've ever heard. If they believe that, then Tory was right. Their coach *is* working them too hard.

"Why would they think that?" I ask.

"Because Sam Romero told them to."

My entire world shifts. Everything looks off kilter. The desks rest at an odd angle. The whiteboards hang crookedly on the wall. Even Caro's face on Tory's phone looks distorted, like I'm viewing her through the bottom of a glass.

"Why?" I say. "Why would he do that?" This is not a question I expect an answer to.

"Well, yeah," Tory says. "No one knows about that part of it."

On the phone's screen, Caro's gaze goes to Tory, then Tory turns toward me. "We're thinking you might know why."

My mind goes back to that first secret practice session, the one where Sam said, "You used to be so ..." So *what*? Even now, I can hear the frustration in his voice. What did he mean by that? Did he really think I joined speech to trick everyone? Couldn't he see how truly awful I was, that I wasn't faking? But if I wasn't faking, does that mean he was? All this time? And from the very start? I think of that quote from *Hamlet*:

To thine own self be true.

I did a little reading about Hamlet after Sam threw that quote at me. Sure, it could mean be yourself. But in Shakespeare's day, it meant looking out for your best interests. Was Sam doing that all along?

I feel like a punch line to a joke I don't quite understand.

On the screen, Caro's face flickers.

"I'm losing battery power, and it's almost time for the first round," Tory says. "So we don't know why Romero did any of this. Question is, what are we going to do now?"

I shrug, but Tory won't let me get away with that.

"I'll tell you what we're going to do. You." She points to me. "Are going to be Winnetka's worst nightmare. They don't have anyone strong in prose, not without Romero. I'm predicting you'll make the finals."

Caro squeaks, but Tory cuts the connection. She's all business and stares at me hard. But that look? I can't recall when it shifted, when unworthy became something else, something more. Something ... worthy?

Then Tory takes me by the shoulders and propels me toward the door.

"Showtime," she says. "Let's go prove Winnetka right."

———

WE REACH our table with enough time to grab our scripts and fill our water bottles. The thought of drinking makes my stomach churn. Or maybe that was seeing Caro on Tory's phone. Or finding out about Sam. I don't know. All I know is if I take a sip, I'll spit it all back up again. I set my bottle on my chair and tuck my coat over it. Then I reach for my script.

The table is clear, nothing but its smooth surface meets my fingertips. No neatly typed scene. No forest green construction paper. Nothing. My stomach churns harder. My face goes red hot, like I have a fever.

"My script," I murmur, the words barely leaving my mouth.

"Hm?" Tory doesn't even glance from her note cards.

"My script," I say. "It's gone."

Her head jerks up. "What?"

I point to the table. "I left it right here."

"No. No. On the floor, maybe." She ducks down, and her head

vanishes beneath the table. A moment later, she pops back up. "Ryan, have you seen—?"

"Looking for something?" A chorus of voices echo across the area.

Opposite us, the Winnetka girls stand. The one in the middle, Annika, fans herself with a script backed with dark green construction paper. *My script.* I'm sure of it.

Ryan shoots from his chair so fast, it crashes into the table behind us. He sprints across the common area. I think he might even leap over a table. The Winnetka girls divide my script, each taking a few pages. They run, two down one hallway, the other splitting off toward the stairwell. By the time Ryan reaches the other side, there's no sense following any of the girls. Even if he could catch one of them, what good would a partial script do?

"It'll be okay," Tory says.

I shake my head. I have no words, no way to describe what's just happened and what it's done to my insides. In a few minutes, when the first round starts, I'll have no words there either. The Winnetka girls ran off with them.

Ryan returns, head down, panting hard.

"How did this happen?" Tory growls these words. Even though I see everything through a haze of panic, she sounds fiercer than ever before. "Weren't you sitting here the whole time?" she asks.

"Yeah, well." He stares at his shoes. "I was talking to someone."

"Someone who?"

His gaze darts toward the hall where one of the Winnetka girls vanished.

"Oh, don't tell me," Tory says. "Really? What have I said about fraternizing with the enemy?"

"I didn't think—"

"Seriously, you didn't?" She rubs her hands across her face, then smooths her hair back, securing a few stray pieces with a bobby pin. "We can tell Henderson," she says. "This has got to get them disqualified, maybe even suspended for the rest of the season."

"Maybe," Ryan says, then he focuses on me. "Jolia, look, I'm sorry. I don't know what I was ... I mean, I'm really sorry."

I know he is. His face is all crumpled. His eyes look so sad, and damp, like maybe he's about to cry. Instead, he shoves his hands into his pockets and stares at the ceiling. His Adam's apple bobs once, twice.

"Now what?" I say. "Should I tell Mr. Henderson I can't compete?" The thought fills me with relief. After everything, this feels like the best solution.

Tory makes a face like I suggested we run through the school naked. "Are you kidding? You go to your first round and you compete."

My mouth falls open. I point to the spot where my script was. "I don't—"

"Need it," Tory finishes. "Did you, or did you not, run through it five times on Thursday without even glancing at it?"

"Yes, but—"

"But nothing. It's not a crutch."

Or a prop. Not even a shield. I must do battle unarmed.

Tory takes me by the shoulders. "You can do this. I know you can. Even better, when you walk in without your script, you will totally freak everyone out. Don't worry if you flub a line. Just be all Jane on her stool and you'll be fine."

Ryan gives my arm an awkward pat. "You can do it."

We walk down the hall, toward the rooms being used for the tournament. That awful feeling, the one where you know you've left something behind, but can't figure out what, follows me to the classroom. There are so many things I don't have—Sam, Caro, my script—that I'm not sure which one I should be looking for.

Chapter 15

DESPITE TORY'S PEP TALK, I walk into my first round in a daze. I sink into my seat and turn my mind toward *Jane Eyre*. Or try to. Behind me comes a snicker. I swivel in my seat, just slightly, and catch sight of a Winnetka girl. She's never done prose before, I'm sure of it. This must be part of the Big 9 shake up before sub-sectionals.

"Lose something?" she says in a voice both too quiet and too mean for a whisper.

I pretend not to hear and jerk toward the front of the classroom.

Bottled up tears touch the corners of my eyes. A wrong word, a wrong look, a wrong thought will send me over the edge, I'm sure of it. With Tory, I was okay. Here alone, I feel empty, betrayed, friendless.

I am Jane on her stool.

Even as I ache, I can't stop the other thoughts, the ones that tell me I can use this hurt, have it lace my words, and come through in my piece, for everyone to feel. It's like a mini-Tory has planted herself in my brain and is feeding me advice. But it's good advice. When the judge calls my name first, I almost smile.

I am ready.

———

AFTER MY THIRD ROUND, I feel as though I've been squeezed through one of those old-fashioned contraptions they used to wring the water out of clothes. There's nothing left to me. If you hung me on the line to dry, I'd just flap on the wind, nearly see-through.

I search for Tory, but Ryan says her last round of extemporaneous speaking has run over.

"But you know," he says, "they posted the finals for prose already."

"Did you make the list?"

"Yeah, but that's not why I mentioned it." He looks me up and down. There's something different in his expression, a glimmer of something I've never seen in his eyes. "You better go check."

"Why?"

He just grins, then locks his lips together with an imaginary key. Oh, God, that really does look dorky.

I head down the hallway, swimming against the tide of kids coming from their last rounds. Not as many people crowd the lists of scores, so I check those first, searching for my name, then blinking several times when I see the numbers next to it:

1, 2, 1

That can't be right. I came in first *twice*? I trace a line from my name to the scores, just to double check, but the numbers don't change. My heart thumps hard. Scores that good can mean only one thing. I'm not sure I'm ready to face that. I'm not sure I have a choice.

Like a zombie, I meander farther down the hallway. Other kids bump me. One knocks my shoulder so hard, I spin around. I hear that same snicker and then see the retreating form of a Winnetka girl. The finalist list isn't that far away, but my steps don't seem to get me any closer, until all at once, I'm there.

Before I can check, a teacher emerges from a room and tapes another list to the wall, this one for extemporaneous speaking. That's easier to deal with, so I scan the names there first. I'm not surprised to find Tory near the top.

I need to check prose. I need to know. I inch closer, passing other lists, my eyes searching for Fremont names and one Winnetka name I probably shouldn't look for. But I can't help it. Each time I pass a list, I check for *Romero, Sam*.

Nothing. He's not even listed in great speeches. The tournament where Sam doesn't final is the one he doesn't attend. He's not here today. I sigh with equal amounts of relief and sadness.

The next list is the one for prose. I can't put it off any longer, so I take one giant step and land in front of it. My heartbeat goes into overtime. For a second, it's like I've forgotten how to read. I see the list of names—all five of them—and slowly the jumbled letters sort themselves out.

What I read, right there at the top is:

Cuppernull, Jolia

I can't believe Tory's prediction came true, but there's the proof. The name below mine is:

Dinsmore, Ryan

Then my eyes lock on the last name on the list. My racing heart stops so hard, it feels like someone hit me in the chest.

Romero, Sam

I spin around, but if Sam's in the area, he's well hidden. He's not only at the tournament, but he's back in prose? My thoughts whirl. How can that be? I think about what Tory and Caro told me, about how Winnetka thought I was a ringer. Could Sam being back in prose have something to do with that?

Before I can sort out an answer, Mr. Henderson finds me.

"Jolia!" he says. "Congratulations. Your progress this season has been … impressive." He gives me an odd look. I wonder if Tory's told him about my stolen script or if he has some sort of teacher sense that alerts him to these things.

"Make sure you eat and drink at lunch today," he continues. "It's easy to get nervous and not do that. I'd hate to see you faint during the final round."

Yeah, I'd hate that too.

I nod and say thank you, and because it looks dorky hanging out by the finalists' lists, I head for the common area and the Fremont team.

———

I'M PRETTY SURE the tournament organizers picked the tiniest, stuffiest room for the prose finals. The wall between our room and the one next door is a folding wall, thin and creaky—and we hear everything going on in there.

The judge shoves open the connecting door, asks if theirs is an actual final round or if they're just goofing off. All at once, silence fills the air. The judge sighs, leans against the now closed door, and gives the four out of the five finalists a relieved smile.

"That's better," she says.

And the fifth finalist? Well, he isn't here. With five minutes before the start, my gaze won't leave the threshold no matter how hard I tell myself not to wait for him—not to *worry* for him.

Because now I see everything clearly. The secret coaching was a setup—one I fell for without suspecting a thing. Sure, Sam coached me, but he also knows *everything* about how I read my piece—all my strengths, all my weaknesses. He's heard me so many times, he could almost perform *Jane Eyre* without a script.

I can't compete with that. I can't compete against Sam Romero. I have the feeling he knows this.

"Hey." Ryan leans in and taps my arm. He's at the desk next to mine, and while he's no Sam Romero, it's nice to have someone on my side. "I'm here because of you," he says.

"Huh?" My mind is too consumed with Sam to come up with anything witty.

"I rewrote my intro. Like you said, it's about courage, not fear." He shrugs. "The second I did that, I started scoring higher." He holds out a hand. "So, thanks. And good luck."

"You, too," I say and shake his hand.

According to the clock on the wall, the round starts in one minute. The judge checks her watch, then glances at the clock.

"Another minute or two," she says. "Then we'll start."

Three seconds after the minute hand reaches twelve, Sam flies into the room. His hair is on end, his cheeks flushed, his eyes dark and dull. They don't look like summer at all. He takes the seat closest to the door, as if he plans to make a quick getaway after the round. If he wants to look at me, he'll have to turn around.

Instead, he stares straight ahead, hands clenched on either side of the desk, a folder lying in the middle. My guess is *Flowers for Algernon* is somewhere inside. If he reads that, first place is his. Ryan opens his mouth, but before I can hear what he's going to say, the judge starts the round.

"Welcome, spectators and especially participants, to the serious prose interpretation final round," she says. "These are the best of the best of our prose contestants today. So, spectators, enjoy! And participants? Try not to be too nervous."

Despite her words, a very nervous laugh ripples through the room.

"Order of speaking is determined by random draw. First up, G-22."

Sam stands, opens the folder, and the rustle of paper fills the room. From where I sit, I see script pages backed with different colors, gold, blue—and forest green. He takes his place at the front of the room and starts his introduction.

At first, all I can see is that green construction paper—the color of summer, of oak leaves, of his eyes. I don't understand what he's saying, or maybe I just don't believe it. His introduction comes out garbled. Only when Sam starts the piece does the enormity of what he's doing hits home. He's not reading from *Flowers for Algernon*.

Sam Romero is reading the Jane on her stool scene from *Jane Eyre*.

Ryan turns his head toward me, his eyes wide with shock. He mouths the word, "What?"

I give my head a slight shake. I don't know what's going on. I don't know why Sam would steal my piece. I really don't know why he's reading it so horribly, or at least horribly for Sam.

When he finishes, I feel like Jane on the stool, only with it kicked out from under me. What am I going to do when it's my turn?

The judge writes comments on Sam's critique sheet, her pen scratching the paper. In the pause between Sam and the next speaker, Ryan leans across the aisle.

"What was that?" he whispers.

"I have no idea." And I don't. Blood pounds in my ears and makes all my thoughts blur.

"Do you think he had those girls steal your script?"

The Sam I know would never do that. But maybe I never really knew him.

"I was in the second round with him." Ryan's whispered words are urgent. "And he read *Algernon*, so whatever it is, he did it on purpose." Ryan utters a few words I'm glad the judge doesn't hear. "Don't worry. He was lousy. You'll blow him out of the water."

I barely hear this, because my mind latches on to that one phrase ...*he did it on purpose.*

That's because Sam did. He won't look at me, so I'm not sure what's going on. But I'm certain about this. Sam Romero is trying to throw the final round. He's *trying* to lose. On purpose. As soon as I have this thought, another one slams into me. *I really wish he hadn't.* Because I don't want to win that way.

"All right," the judge says. "Next up is—" She draws a piece of paper from her desk. "—L-3."

I sink back in my chair, relieved I don't have to speak right after Sam. That would be too weird. The judge would think we're crazy, but she'll probably think that anyway once I stand up and read the exact same scene.

Ryan reads third. In the middle of his piece, he stumbles. His gaze goes straight to Sam, as if Sam reading *Jane Eyre* was meant to mess with everyone's head. Whether it was or not, Ryan is rattled. The mistake isn't fatal, he recovers, and the entire room is leaning forward by the time he reads the shark attack. Still, it's not his best performance. When he collapses at his desk, he exhales another word that I'm glad the judge doesn't hear. "That sucked," he says right before the judge calls my number.

I never have the chance to contradict him. I stand and shake out my skirt. Before heading to the front of the room, I touch my scarf for good luck. Murmurs fill the air when everyone realizes I'm reading the same exact scene as Sam. I feel my two phantom front teeth, but the sensation fades the further I get into the scene. By the end, I am Jane Eyre. When I finish, the judge nods at me, and I walk back to my desk on wobbly legs. I melt into the seat. Whatever happens next doesn't matter quite so much as this: It's over.

Sam still stares straight ahead, but Ryan's full attention is on me.

"Wow," is all he says.

———

IN THE AUDITORIUM, I'm surrounded by the Fremont team. The place is buzzing with chatter, the squeals pitched higher, the conversations more frantic. During the day, it's dawned on me that the Big 9 tournament is a huge deal. It's not sub-sectionals or regionals, but for some kids, it's even more important. We're competing against the schools in our conference. Fremont isn't the only team with a rival like Winnetka. If not for my own drama-filled day, I could've enjoyed the other ones playing out around me. Speech really could be a reality TV show.

No one from the Winnetka team approaches us. I crane my neck and think I see Sam. He's sitting on the opposite side of the auditorium where the Winnetka team has gathered, in an aisle seat, as if—yet again—he needs to make a quick getaway.

Tory stands in the center of our group, her eyes lit with the scandal of the serious prose final round. "I can't believe he read your piece," she says for maybe the fifth or sixth time. I've lost count.

"I think he did it on purpose," I say.

"Well, duh," comes Tory's reply. "Of course he did. They stole your script. Besides," she adds, "I'm pretty sure this disqualified him."

I shake my head, frustrated Tory doesn't see what I do. "I mean the final round. I think he threw it. On purpose."

"Romero would never do that. His coach would kill him. He's their ticket to state."

"Then why would he get himself disqualified with *Jane Eyre* when he could win with *Algernon*?"

Tory makes a face. "Who says he would've won?"

"Have you heard him?" Deep down, I know: no one reads like Sam does when he reads *Flowers for Algernon*. He becomes the main character, Charlie, makes you feel the heartbreak. He would've won.

Tory shrugs and glances toward the Winnetka team. "Then ... why?"

"I think it means he likes her," Kaitlin says.

Tory scowls at her.

"Well, I do." Kaitlin crosses her arms over her chest. "And it's not like you know what it means."

Tory taps her shoe against the floor, a jittery sound that tells me she's nervous.

"You can count me out of prose," Ryan says as he plops down behind us. "I choked right in the middle of my piece."

"It wasn't that bad," I say, "more like a stumble."

Tory narrows her eyes at me, then shoots her twin a look filled with daggers. "Oh, really?"

"I'm telling you, Romero did it on purpose." Ryan holds up his hands as if to ward her off. "And it worked. It totally messed with my head."

"All of you take note," Tory says. "I don't want to hear the name Sam Romero for the rest of the day."

Ryan rolls his eyes. Kaitlin giggles. Before Tory can issue another order, the Mankato East speech team coach takes the stage. Predictably, Tory scoots past me twice—once for discussion (second place) and once for extemporaneous speaking (first). I wonder if the Dinsmores have an entire room devoted to all the trophies Tory and Ryan bring home.

When the names for great speeches echo through the auditorium, I expect to hear Sam's. Kids on the Winnetka team shift in their seats like they expect the same thing. There are no chants of *Ro-me-o, Ro-me-o*. The stage seems wrong without Sam on it.

At last, the coach announces the serious prose winners. Tory clutches my arm, like she's the one waiting for her name to be called.

"What about Ryan?" I whisper.

"Not a chance," she says. "He blew it."

Ryan smacks her in the back of the head just as his name is called for third place. I clap until my hands ache.

"It really was just a stumble," I say to Tory, but I don't think she can hear me over her own cheers.

Second place goes to a girl from Mankato East. The home team goes wild. Tory reestablishes her grip on my arm and holds on even tighter. Ryan leans forward. Next to me, Kaitlin seems to vibrate. I hate for everyone to be so disappointed when my name isn't called.

Up on stage, the Mankato East coach consults the piece of paper in his hand. "And the winner of the serious prose interpretation category is … Jolia Cuppernull from Fremont High School! Congratulations, Jolia!"

There's a roaring in my ears. I can't tell if it's coming from inside or outside of my head. Tory yanks me up while Kaitlin pushes from behind. Together they shove me from the row and into the aisle. I turn back to stare at them.

"Get up there!" Tory yells. "Go get your trophy!"

My legs have all the strength of wet noodles. I stumble down the aisle, a sea of applause crashing around me. The stairs look steep, but somehow, I climb them. Then I'm up on the stage. I know it's probably the wrong thing to do—that it will probably send me into a fit of stage fright—but I look out at the audience.

From up here, everything's so clear. I see the battle lines drawn between the teams—Winnetka to my right, Fremont to my left. Somehow I ended up in the middle.

I search for Sam. He's not clapping, but relief fills his face. He's the reason I'm up on this stage. Not just because he threw the final round, but because he believed in me from the start.

The coach hands me the first place trophy. The thing is huge. I'm not ready for its weight, and my arms sag when he lets go. A ripple of friendly laughter flows through the audience. After I shake the coach's hand, I hold the trophy high above my head, the way I've seen everyone else do. All the Fremont kids jump up and down. Kaitlin screams. Ryan gives me a double thumbs up.

I can't help glancing at Sam. He has his hands braced against the arms of his seat as if he's ready to bolt from the auditorium. An idea grips my mind: I can't let him do that.

I take a shaky step down the stairs. Instead of crossing in front of the stage, I head straight up the aisle in front of me. I head straight for the Winnetka team.

A hush falls over the auditorium. The Mankato East coach doesn't continue with the next category. No one says anything. When I'm halfway to his seat, Sam's eyes go huge. He gives his head a slight shake, but I keep going.

I'm tired of not speaking up, because, sometimes, that's the same as lying. And I can't lie about Sam. The moment before I reach him, he stands. I hug the trophy to me—a quick hello and then goodbye. Then I thrust it at him.

"Here," I say. "You earned this."

I let the trophy go. Sam has no choice. If he doesn't make a grab for it, the trophy will crash to the floor. He catches it and then, somehow, my wrist, too. His grip is so gentle, I know I can slip away. But I don't—or can't. Both of us are speechless, maybe everyone in the auditorium is, but they've faded into the background. It's just me and Sam and the glint of the golden trophy between us.

We can't stand like this forever. I lean in and break the spell with a soft kiss on his cheek.

"Thank you," I whisper.

He lets me slip away.

Without looking back, I walk up the aisle. I pick up my coat in the common area, and then I push through the lobby doors and head outside. I tip my face toward the afternoon sun and take in its warmth. Tory was right. It was a good omen. With the sun at my back, I go find the Fremont bus.

Chapter 16

ON THE BUS, I take a seat near the back and pull out my phone. Even though I'm out of practice, I could text Caro in my sleep. I peck out two words and send them to her:

Thank you.

I clutch my phone, but I don't expect it to vibrate. It doesn't.

From the school, kids emerge, fanning out, each looking for the bus to take them home. Among the crowd, golden trophies glint in the sun. I don't see Sam. I think maybe that's just as well.

Everyone is really quiet as they file onto the bus. A few kids nod, but most shuffle past, looking at everything but me. I figure my fate is sealed. Any moment, Tory will charge onto the bus and beat me with her own first place trophy.

Instead, she just flops down in the seat in front of mine. "You okay?" she asks.

I shrug.

"I figured as much."

I don't say anything.

After a moment, Tory says, "You know Sam Romero."

This is not a question. I suppose the trophy—not to mention the kiss—gave the whole thing away. But Tory deserves an answer. She deserves the truth.

"Up until a couple of weeks ago, Sam was secretly coaching me."

I never thought I'd be the one to shock Tory speechless, but it sure looks that way. Her mouth hangs open a little, both eyebrows raised.

"We live in the same neighborhood," I say. "We were friends, when we were little."

Mr. Henderson climbs onto the bus, his gaze scanning all of us. He has to make sure we're all here before the driver shuts the door for the last time. When he reaches me, his eyes narrow. Then he pulls a cell phone from his coat pocket.

"Am I in trouble?" I ask Tory.

"Honestly? I think maybe we all are."

"Did you tell Mr. Henderson about my script?"

Tory makes a face. "Yeah, that conversation didn't go as planned."

"Didn't he care?" I can't believe that, and I hope Tory tells me what he said.

"Oh, he *cared*. But he started asking all sorts of questions. I think." She glances toward the front of the bus. "He's talking to the Winnetka coach now."

The bus rumbles beneath us, and something about it forces words from my mouth. Once I start, the whole story comes out— or at least most of it. I don't tell Tory about the rink rats, but she hears all the rest, my friendship with Sam, the secret coaching, and especially the reason for it. The miles flash by with my words and by the time we're halfway home, I know I owe her an apology.

"You were right," I say, "I didn't want to be on the speech team. But it was either that or fail."

A frown creases Tory's brow, one reminiscent of the days when I was unworthy. I hate that we're back there, but that's the least I deserve. "I'm sorry," I say. "I really—"

She holds up a hand, stopping me. "No, it's ... why would Romero tell everyone you're all that in the first place?"

I shake my head and shake a stray tear from my eye. "I don't know."

"And then coach you," she finishes. She leans back against the window, closes her eyes. "I'm so glad this season is almost over. I am so sick of hearing the name Sam Romero."

My sigh comes out heavy with sadness.

Tory's eyes fly open. "Really? After all this time? Didn't I tell you they call him Romeo for a reason?"

With her words, my heart starts aching all over again. "You did."

Everyone is silent when we arrive at school. One by one, we trek from the bus and into the speech classroom to drop off whatever we won't need until Monday.

"Ryan and Tory?" Mr. Henderson says. "A word with you."

They huddle around his desk. The look Mr. Henderson gives the rest of us makes it clear: *No eavesdropping.*

But when I reach the door, Mr. Henderson adds, "Jolia, why don't you wait in the hall."

Kaitlin and Savannah look almost as scared as I feel. My heart thumps. I pull off my mittens because my hands are sweating like crazy. I lean against the wall outside the classroom. Kaitlin and Savannah say goodbye. I'm alone, with nothing—no script, no trophy. Voices come from the classroom—mostly Mr. Henderson's—but I can't hear what they're saying. Then, louder, I hear:

"Ms. Cuppernull? You can come in now."

Mr. Henderson is at his desk, Ryan and Tory in front of it.

There's an empty spot next to her, a spot meant for me, I can tell. I inch forward until I'm standing next to Tory.

"Can I ask you about today?" he says, although it's not so much a real question as a *teacher* question. There isn't an option not to answer.

"Why did you give your trophy to Sam Romero?"

"Is there a rule against giving your trophy away?" I'm pretty sure the trophies don't belong to the school, not after watching Tory and Ryan lug them home week after week. Ryan snorts. And although I can't see her, I'm pretty sure Tory rolls her eyes.

Mr. Henderson's lips twitch. "I don't think there's an actual rule, but most people like to keep their very first, first place trophy."

Something sharp pings against my heart. No matter how right I thought I was, part of me wishes I'd kept the trophy, to have something to show my parents and especially my brother Derek.

"So," he says, "we're back to why."

So I explain about knowing Sam long before speech team, and how he offered to coach me. And because I figured I couldn't get any worse, his coaching might help.

"But now I don't know," I say. "I mean after today with my script—"

"Tory explained how the Winnetka team thought you were a plant and about your stolen script. You know, I'm required to file a copy of all scripts before each tournament."

Tory exhales and slaps her forehead.

"I might have been able to get you a replacement," Mr. Henderson says.

Now he tells us? Shock rolls through me, and I sprout a new crop of sweat like I'm gearing up for the final round all over again. I'm seriously considering making a run for the bathroom. Except we're not excused, not yet.

"On the drive back," Mr. Henderson continued, "I called the Winnetka coach, and we had a long chat."

I wait, hoping he'll shed some light on what Sam did and, more importantly, why.

"According to her, Sam admitted to coaching you, but refused to say anything about today's final round."

"Oh." I feel myself sag.

"What about Jolia's script?" Tory asks. "I don't think it's fair—"

Mr. Henderson holds up a hand, silencing her. "I agree and so does the Winnetka coach. She will deal with it."

Tory's brow crinkles in disappointment and outrage. If she could, I bet she'd storm into Winnetka High School and demand justice.

"Besides," Mr. Henderson continues, "we discovered today that Jolia doesn't need her script. But we still need to decide what to do about sub-sectionals."

I perk up, my heart hammering. I never thought past today, past the final round, and what that might mean. Tory reaches over and gives my hand a quick squeeze.

"If the only thing that mattered was winning, I'd slot you for prose and start prepping for state right now."

State? I give my head a slight shake. Today could've been a fluke. I'm not ready for state. Even as I think this, Tory whispers, "Told you so."

"But I can't let this go unpunished. You should've come to me, or asked Tory or Ryan to help you."

I nod.

"I really have no choice, Jolia," Mr. Henderson says. "You're suspended from participating in one tournament."

The pieces fall into place. If I don't compete in sub-sectionals—the next tournament—I can't move on to the regional tournament. I can't move on to state. Which is better? Winning? Or honesty? I think I know. And I think—no, I'm positive—I'm okay with that.

166

"What about Tory and Ryan?" I ask. If they're suspended too? Guilt rushes through me, and I rush my words. "They didn't do anything wrong, not really. They only tried to help—"

"And both the Winnetka coach and I feel that the co-captains on each team fostered an atmosphere of unhealthy rivalry instead of spirited competition."

Ryan snorts again. Tory sighs. They've heard this before, clearly.

"And then there's the question about hacking."

Next to me, Tory stiffens. *This*, they haven't heard.

"All three of you know that's a serious offense, right?"

Oh, God. My vision blurs. I blink, even though that will make the tears spill down my cheeks. I can't wipe them away, either, because I'm clutching my mittens in one hand and Tory's with the other. From her grip, I can tell, she's not letting go.

"Don't blame Jolia," Tory blurts out. "She told us to stop."

Well, I did, and I didn't, but the second I open my mouth, Mr. Henderson holds up a hand.

"The Winnetka coach and I agree that the captains from both teams will be suspended from competition for the rest of the season."

Tory's fingers go limp in my hand.

"I had to think long and hard about expelling you from the team, but I feel my and Ms. Cabera's ambitions for our separate teams may have played a role in this." Mr. Henderson sighs, like this hurts him too. "I expect the two of you to attend practice, coach the other team members, and support the team at the remaining tournaments."

With their faces downcast, Tory and Ryan nod.

"Could I do that too?" I ask him. "Coach, and help, and support?"

Mr. Henderson's gaze surveys me. He looks more pleased than surprised by my question, although he still doesn't look all that happy. "Yes, I think the team would appreciate it. I think Tory and Ryan would to."

They don't move, and I'm not sure what they think.

Mr. Henderson dismisses us. He's subdued. We all are. I shrug on my coat again, but pushing my arms through the sleeves feels extra hard. Ryan and Tory pick up their trophies like they weigh ten pounds each. Tory examines hers carefully as if it's some artifact that belongs in a museum. We're at the door when Mr. Henderson calls out one last time.

"I'll be putting final grades into the system this weekend, Ms. Cuppernull. You might want to go online and check yours."

And that is all he'll say about that.

———

WE DON'T SPEAK, not until we reach the lobby. There, we huddle in a corner. Tory pulls out her cell phone, a deep line forming between her brows.

"You guys," I say. "I'm sorry." Somehow, this feels like it's all my fault. From the moment I agreed to Sam's secret coaching, I tipped the first domino, and this is the fallout.

"We're lucky." Tory holds up the phone. "Mom says so."

"What? She knows?" Ryan lurches forward. "You're lucky it's not going on your record," he reads. "Crap—she didn't actually say 'crap.' That was me."

"She'll say more than that when we get home." Tory shoves the phone into her messenger bag.

She's about to stand, but it's like her legs decide to stop working. She crumples against me, her sobs so strong, they shake both of us, and loosen the tears flooding my eyes. Ryan fumbles with the trophies, sets them down, picks them up, his hands all nervous, like he wants to fix his sister, but doesn't know where to start. So I hold her and let her cry. The sobs slow until—finally—they're hiccups, then haggard breaths.

"The worst thing?" Tory says. "Facing everyone at the tournaments. How am I going to explain? It's going to be so embarrassing."

"More embarrassing than failing speech?" I ask.

A heartbeat passes, then another. Just when I'm afraid Tory will shove me into the trophy cases, she hugs me tighter, shaking, only this time, with laughter.

"I'll be there with you guys," I add.

She pulls back. "Really?"

"Promise."

She plucks at the scarf I'm wearing. "And then there's this."

"You want me to knit you a scarf?"

"I want you to teach me. I'm going to have lots of time on my hands."

I turn to Ryan. "How about you?"

"There's lots of girls in this club, right?"

"Oh, yeah."

He shrugs. "Why the hell not."

A car horn sounds and I walk them outside. A very blond, older version of Tory shoves open the passenger door of a Volvo station wagon. She points to the front seat, and Tory meekly slides inside. It's going to be a bumpy ride home.

I don't have time to even wave. At that moment, our car pulls into the parking lot. That must mean Mr. Henderson called Mom and Dad too. And yes, it looks like I'm in for my own bumpy ride.

————

AT HOME, Mom meets us at the front door. Dad hasn't said anything for the entire ride—except that Mr. Henderson called them. All the way home, I'm convinced I'll throw up. Now that I'm here, I'm pretty sure I will.

But Mom is smiling. And when we reach the den, so is Dad.

"Mr. Henderson said you won first place." And with this, Mom gives me a huge hug. All I can do is nod.

"Did he tell you why I don't have a trophy?" I squeak out at last.

Mom and Dad exchange glances. "Yes," Dad says. "Something about a boy from another school."

"It was Sam."

"*Oh.*" Mom raises her eyebrows. "Sam."

"It wasn't right," I say, "to get coaching from the rival team."

"It's not how it's usually done," Dad agrees.

"Not at all," Mom echoes.

I wonder: what on earth is going on. I'm waiting for the grounding, the lecture, or ... something. So at last, I just ask.

"Am I in trouble?"

Mom holds her finger and thumb about an inch apart. "Maybe this much."

"Grounded?"

Dad holds up seven fingers. "This many days."

I realize I've been grounded for spring break, the same spring break where I have zero plans because Caro isn't talking to me, Derek is out of the country, and there isn't a tournament until after Easter.

After Easter.

"I told Mr. Henderson I'd like to support the team," I say.

"He mentioned that and seemed very impressed."

The crazy thing is, I do want to support the team. I want to scope out the competition—for next year. Do I want to see Sam? My heart squeezes tight and won't let me answer that question.

"So your mom and I agree," Dad says. "On one condition."

I hold my breath.

Mom and Dad settle on the couch. Dad wraps an arm around her shoulder, like he does when we watch movies together. They look all set to see a show.

"Will you do your piece for us?" he asks.

"You want to hear *Jane Eyre*?"

"Can't wait," Mom says. "I hear it's a prize-winning piece."

"I might be a little shaky," I say, "I don't have my script."

"According to Mr. Henderson, you don't need one." Dad winks.

So they know all about that, too! I clear my throat, think about being all Jane on her stool, and perform *Jane Eyre* for the fifth time that day.

As punishments go, this isn't so bad.

Chapter 17

MONDAY AFTER SPRING BREAK, I freeze at the cafeteria door. The first thing I see is Jeremy, back at his usual table, surrounded by all his jock friends. A few girls occupy the table where Caro and I used to sit, but she isn't one of them. It looks like we've lost our claim to that space. Not that it was much of a claim. Not that there's an "us" to claim it anymore.

I feel hollow inside and not at all like eating whatever they're serving today. I turn to leave when I hear my name.

"Jolia!" Tory waves an arm over her head. At her table, I see Ryan, Kaitlin, Savannah—and Caro. Tory shoots me a look, the same sort she'd send my way when I froze in front of the camera. She tugs Caro by the sleeve—which must mean she's serious about something—and half-drags her across the cafeteria.

When Tory grabs my sleeve, I realize that something is me. In the girls' bathroom, she bars the way out, arms crossed, fierce debater face fully on.

"Listen," she says. "After all the work I've done, you two are not leaving until you make up."

Work? As in inviting Caro to sit at the speech table? That sounds like a very Sherlock Holmes thing to do. I know Caro well enough to be certain it wasn't her idea. I cast Caro a look. She gives her head a tiny shake, like she's not entirely sure what's going on either.

"You." Tory points at Caro. "Need to think of someone other than yourself, especially if that someone is so loyal she keeps all your secrets, even when you're being a first class bitch."

Caro opens her mouth, but I get there first. "Hey! That's not—"

"And you." Tory rounds on me. "Need to stop being a doormat. If someone is stepping all over you, you need to tell them it freaking hurts." She exhales. "I was totally going to steal Jolia from you," she says now to Caro. "But I can't do that. After everything, I can tell she still thinks you're her best friend." She raises her hands, lets them fall, and turns to leave.

I can't let her do that. "But what about that bossy, know-it-all friend?" I say.

Tory halts, her shoulders tense, like she might shatter into pieces.

"You tell her thanks," Caro says.

"Then maybe suggest she take up a relaxing hobby," I add. "Like knitting."

Something happens then. I know Tory won't shatter. Neither will I. Neither will Caro. It's not like we're piecing together the splinters of our friendship. It's like we're creating something new, maybe something even better. So, of course, I have to say something profound.

"I'm starving."

Caro laughs. "I got a ton of stuff from home. My mom had an order cancel at the last minute. We have food for days."

"Pastries?" I ask.

"You know it."

"You've got to try her mom's baking," I tell Tory as we head out the bathroom door, but her expression is blank, like she hasn't heard. She pins me in place with an index finger to my shoulder.

"Wait," Tory says. "What about speech? Did you pass?"

Caro stares open mouthed. "You were failing a class? *You?*"

"It was pretty epic," I say.

"Well?" Tory taps her foot.

"I got a B."

"That's it?"

"That's ... really good," I say. A twenty nine out of thirty on my last speech put me over the top.

"You're going to tell me about this," Caro says. "Right?"

I can't hold in my smile. "In creative storytelling."

"Good. Then I'll tell you how I'm still grounded."

Now Tory grins. "I know both stories." She flips her hair over one shoulder and heads not for the cafeteria, but the courtyard area with all its sunshine.

Caro eyes me. Without a word, we both run after her.

———

IN CREATIVE STORYTELLING, Mrs. Riley lets us use the long table at the back of the room. Caro and I are the only ones attempting a graphic novel. At least for now. A few kids wander by and *oh* and *ah* at Caro's artwork.

"It's more than pretty pictures," Caro tells them. "You have to work with a good storyteller."

And I know she means me.

We talk quietly while we work. Because this is a partner project, no one can demand silence from us. Okay, so maybe we're not discussing the plot for our retelling of *Romeo and Juliet*. Then again, it's possible that we are. Write what you know? I sigh. I think we both know this story, especially when I hear why Caro is grounded.

"Friday before spring break," she says. "I told my mom the truth about Jeremy."

Caro's confession nearly knocks the wind from me. I rub my stomach as if she's actually hit me there. "You mean, she didn't find out? You ... *told* her?"

For a moment, Caro squeezes her eyes shut. "I hated lying all the time. When it was just about Jeremy, it wasn't so bad. But when she started in on you, I just couldn't do it anymore." She swallows hard. "My mom went ballistic. But the worst of it? She already knew."

"She *knew*?"

"Since the winter carnival, and everything she said about you, she didn't mean a word."

"She was waiting to see how long it would take you to break?" I suggest.

Caro makes a face. "Pretty much."

"Whoa. Remind me never to mess with your mom."

"Are you kidding? She adores you. She heard about your first place speech thingy, and now she wants me to join the team next year." Caro rolls her eyes.

We work in silence for a while until she adds, "Here's the funny thing. It was worth it."

"What was?"

"Telling her." She adds a bit of shading to the Juliet she's sketching, and it's like tears flow through her fingertips. This Juliet looks so sad we must find a way to use her in our graphic novel. "I feel like myself again."

To thine own self be true. The words make me think of Sam, and my chest goes tight, like I've laced it up with shoes strings and pulled hard. I've tried not to think of him at all but haven't been having much luck with that.

Later, Mrs. Riley comes over to inspect our progress. Caro has placed her sad Juliet on an apartment complex balcony. I'm wondering about that line from *Hamlet* and how we might make it the theme of our story.

Mrs. Riley studies Caro's drawings, then flips through our storyboard. "Are you girls going to give this retelling a happy ending?"

Caro and I exchange glances. At the same time, we both shake our heads. Mrs. Riley laughs and moves on.

"But I think," Caro whispers, "Juliet is going to be just fine."

"Me, too," I say. "Me, too."

Chapter 18

IT'S the first Sunday in April, the day after sub-sectionals. We—Tory, Ryan, and I—worked with the team all week, especially Ben, Kaitlin, and Savannah, since they're all coming back next year. No one said a word about our non-participation in the tournament and, while Fremont is done for the season, Kaitlin placed in the top ten and Ben took home an honorable mention ribbon.

I never saw Sam. Same for Annika and a bunch of the Winnetka girls. Compared to the Big 9 tournament, sub-sectionals was the reality TV episode where nothing really happens.

"Next year," Tory predicted on the bus ride home. "We'll be all set to kick some Winnetka ass."

A text message wakes me this morning. Caro's still grounded—from everything—so I know it's not her. Sam might as well be on a different planet. Who else might text me, and so early, I don't know. I check my phone and find a message from someone I haven't talked to in a while.

What's this about a trophy and grounding? Mom and Dad make no sense. Get on Skype. Now.

WTH. I leave for break and miss all the drama.

Derek! I stumble from bed and boot up my laptop without even brushing my hair. He makes a face when I first pop up on Skype, but he doesn't look much better. Sure, he's tan from spring break in Mexico, where he worked with endangered sea turtles. But he's wearing a stretched out, old T-shirt, and his dorm room is a disaster. There's even a pair of underwear hanging from the Nerf basketball hoop on his doorframe.

"Who said you could do anything interesting while I'm out of the country?" he says.

"I want to hear about your trip," I counter.

"I want to hear how my perfect little sister gets herself grounded for winning first place."

When he puts it like that, it does sound kind of crazy, maybe even more interesting than saving sea turtles (although not nearly as noble). I try to explain, but it's like a big jumbled jigsaw puzzle. He needs all the pieces to see the picture. So I go back to the very beginning, starting with that cold day at the bus stop and the rink rats. He frowns at that.

"Jo," he says, "next time you tell someone. Okay? I'm serious."

But when he hears about Crandall's bike, all he can do is laugh.

Derek looks thoughtful when I finish. He doesn't say anything, so I continue talking.

"I wish I knew," I say, "why Sam did it."

"Why don't you ask him?"

"What?"

"From what I remember, he's a good kid. He might have—okay, maybe he doesn't have a *good* reason." Derek shrugs. "But one that might make sense." He leans close to the camera and lowers his voice. "I'm going to tell you a secret about guys, but you can't tell anyone else, okay?"

I nod, then cross my heart.

He glances around as if he's afraid someone is listening. "Sometimes, when we like a girl, we do stupid stuff."

My cheeks blaze hot. My pre-calc homework is only inches away and I'm sure the heat from my face will set it on fire.

"Give him a chance to explain," Derek says. "You don't have to like the answer, but at least you'll know."

He's right, of course, in the way big brothers almost always are. But Sam wasn't at the last tournament and we're done for the season. I won't see him until next year. Maybe. Maybe Sam will never go out for speech again. Then what?

Unless. I feel a smile spread across my face. I pull back the curtains and catch sight of pale blue sky. It's going to be a perfect day, perfect for the park.

"Got somewhere to go?" Derek asks with his own grin.

"I think I do."

———

ALL MORNING LONG, I stare at my phone. Finally, after lunch, I bring up that strange number, Sam's number, and write:

Jolia: Park in 10?

I don't wait for an answer, but I tuck my script—Sam's script—of *Romeo and Juliet* into my coat pocket.

Outside, the sun warms my face and makes me squint. I blink and feel the soft air against my eyes. Spring is beating back winter, even though speckled piles of snow still line the sidewalk to the park.

In between me and the park bench, a figure steps onto the sidewalk. His shoulders are wide, and he walks like he'd rather be skating. What's a rink rat to do when spring steals all the ice?

In the split second when I realize it's Crandall, and he realizes it's me, his steps stutter. He glances toward the road, like he's thinking about crossing to the other side. He doesn't, but I swear he walks a little faster, not to get *to* me, but to get *past* me.

He brushes by with a strange jerk of his head. He doesn't say anything, and neither do I. When he's gone, and I feel like I can turn my head without him seeing, I stop. I gulp a breath and tell my heart to hush. It's over. I'll never be bothered by a rink rat again.

The air smells like spring, and I breathe in happiness all the way to the park. When I see the bench is empty, everything inside me sinks—my heart, my mood, my hopes. And I sink to the park bench.

I see the brown paper bag first. It's huge. I pretend I don't see the boy who's carrying it. I pull my knees up and rest my chin on them. Only when Sam is a few feet away do I turn my head and peer at him.

His eyes look like summer. My heart starts up again, and this time, I can't tell it to shush. Then he smiles, and I'm as warm as this spring day.

He sits on the bench, placing the bag carefully between us. For a couple of minutes, we both sit there without speaking, but it isn't weird or uncomfortable. In a way, it feels almost like we're seven again, when we first became friends. And in a way, there's something very new about this.

"I suppose you have some questions about—" Sam gazes up at the sky. "Well, everything, I guess."

I do and decide to ask the worst one first. "Did you have, I mean, did you tell … those girls who took my script—"

Sam holds up a hand, stopping me. "You don't have to believe me, but once I heard what they did, I spent the whole day trying to get your script back. I wanted to give it to you before the final round started." He exhales hard and stares at the sky. "That didn't happen." His face turns toward me again. "Not that you needed it."

"I thought I did," I say. "At least at first."

"I never told them to take it."

"This might sound crazy, but I'm kind of glad they did."

Sam cocks his head, like he can't wait to hear what I'll say next.

"You know, not a prop or a crutch."

He laughs, but the sound is nervous. He's still nervous. About me?

"Is that why you read my piece?" I ask.

He nods. "I wanted to … level the playing field."

"But that disqualified you, didn't it?" I know the answer, looked it up over spring break. Reading a different piece in the final round did disqualify him. From the expression on his face now, I can tell: he went into the finals knowing it would.

"I wanted to make up for what they did," he says.

"Can I ask you something that really confuses me?"

"You can ask me anything. I owe you that much."

"Why did you tell everyone on your team that I was a ringer?" That's the other thing I really want to know. At lunch, Tory and Ryan still debate the reasons why, but none of them make sense to me.

"From the summers." His words are quiet, and he waves a hand at the park behind us. "You used to build castles in the air that I swore I could walk through. When I heard you joined the Fremont team, I thought for sure you'd do something like original story-telling, and I told everyone we'd have to watch out for you."

"Those first tournaments must've been kind of a shock." I don't even cringe when I say this.

"Yeah, I couldn't figure out what was up. The team kept asking, especially Annika, and I kept insisting you'd be brilliant. I dug myself in too deep. By the time I knew you weren't faking, everyone on my team thought you were a ringer." He shifts toward me. "Then I thought, why not make it come true? I mean, I knew you had it inside you right from the start. This way, you'd get a trophy, and the team wouldn't think I was crazy. It was the perfect plan."

"Until everything else went crazy."

"Yeah. That."

"I joined so I could pass speech class," I tell him. "Not as some ringer."

"I don't know about that. You blew everyone away at Big 9. My entire team was freaking until they were sure you weren't competing at sub-sectionals."

"I was suspended, but I went as a spectator," I tell him.

"I wasn't even allowed to do that."

"You got in a lot of trouble?"

"We all did, especially the girls who took your script, but I told Ms. Cabera that since I'm the one who actually coached you, I should be the one to take the punishment."

I didn't think I could like Sam more than I already did, but in that moment, I do.

"Wow," I say. "That's … that's brave."

He shrugs off my words. "She suspended them too. I mean, they *stole* your freaking script."

I can't help it. I laugh. And I think this proves my theory. If speech team isn't a reality TV show, it really should be.

"It worked out okay, I guess," Sam says. "At least for me. I got to run in the track invitational yesterday." He pauses, kind of dramatic, too, and doesn't speak until he knows I'm listening hard. "Fremont was there, and I talked to Jeremy Spinner."

"Oh." My heart pounds so hard in my throat, that's all I can force out.

"He's still confused about the whole ringer thing, but me? I'm not confused about anything." Sam stares at me and his eyes remind me of the warmest day of summer. "And we moved last week, so I had to help with that." He rubs his shoulder like just the reminder is painful. "I was unpacking boxes when I got your text."

The spring day turns to ice. Maybe that's why it took so long for Sam to get here because he doesn't live *here* anymore. My chest gets that funny shoelace feeling again—everything is strung too tight. The only thing that comes out is, "You moved."

He points toward his old apartment complex and I follow his finger until it lands on a side street adjacent to the park. I realize he's crossed that line between Winnetka and Fremont. I wonder what that means. For him. For me.

Everything keeping us apart is melting in the sunshine. I think this right up until Sam asks me a question.

"Why were you failing speech?"

"I ... I used to freeze when I stood in front of a classroom," I say. "I used to fake it—you know, be the one with the laser pointer while everyone else talked. But that didn't work in speech class."

"But I don't understand why." He glances at the park behind us, and back at me, the question clear in his eyes. How did the girl who built castles in the air lose her voice?

"Well, I got braces," I begin.

"Wait." Sam holds up a hand while he studies me. It's as if he's trying to reconcile grade-school Jolia with the new one sitting in front of him. "You needed braces?" he asks, his voice genuinely perplexed.

I don't really want to get into The History of My Teeth. Not today, not with the sun so warm and his eyes so green. How even now, those insidious whispers might return—if I let them. I won't.

"It made me ... self-conscious," I say at last. "About how I looked, how my mouth looked. At first, it was just easier not to talk." I tell him how one form of silence led to another, until it was easier not to say anything at all.

"I can see that," he says. "But does the story have a happy ending?"

"I got a B," I tell Sam.

"Really?" He wrinkles his nose. "It should've been an A."

"I had to make up for a lot of zeroes."

"Well, there's always next year."

"Next year?" I try to be cool, but my heart's gone into overtime again.

"I'm thinking you should look into dramatic interpretation," he says. "You have a definite flair for it."

I laugh at this. Me? Dramatic? "How so?"

"Did you or did you not hand me your first place trophy in front of a packed auditorium?"

I think of that soft kiss to his cheek, and my face burns hot. Okay. Maybe he has a point.

"Speaking of which." He reaches into the bag and pulls out the trophy. The gold glints in the sunlight, the shine so bright, I hold up a hand so the glare won't blind me. "I think this is yours," he says.

"Thanks." It's one breathy word and doesn't sound like nearly enough.

"You earned it." Sam won't let me protest that either. He eyes my coat pocket, then pulls one more thing from the paper bag—the script for *Romeo and Juliet*.

"I thought we'd get started early," he says.

"We?"

"Ever hear of duo dramatic interpretation?"

Duo? As in two? As in me and … Sam? "Then—?"

He gives me that crooked grin. "I'm going to Fremont High next fall."

His words steal my breath. I think about that. Speech team—with Sam. School—with Sam. It suddenly looms large, this new territory. I glance at the park. Part of me doesn't want to lose this, those magic summers, or this winter, when we defeated the rink rats. I look at Sam, and I think he feels the same way. He hops from the bench, script tight in his hand. He takes one step, and then another, and I'm right behind him. On the way to the jungle gym, he scoops up a branch. His feet tear up the ground. I follow, the wind stealing my laughter. When we reach the climbing wall, he gives me a boost up.

"This time," he says, "you be Juliet."

But when I reach the top, he's there too. We skip the balcony scene and start with the kiss. My mouth is cold, but his lips are soft and the spring day grows brighter. Okay, so technically, we're not allowed to touch—never mind kiss—during tournament rounds. Still.

That doesn't mean we shouldn't practice.

Author's Note

Within the story, I have tried to stay as close to the rules and regulations of speech team competitions as possible. In some instances, I may have glossed over the finer points, or, for the sake of storytelling, outright changed something. For this, I offer my apologies.

Speech team isn't just for the wildly extroverted. If you have a strong introverted streak or are terminally shy, consider giving speech a try for a season. You might, like Jolia, be surprised what happens.

Acknowledgments

Building a novel is a team effort. Many, many thanks to:

- My critique/writing partner/wordsmith BFF Darcy Vance, who read *The Fine Art of Keeping Quiet* in more than one version and under more than one title.
- Anne Goulish, who did a brilliant job editing the manuscript and schooling me on nonstandard comma usage. All mistakes that remain in the story are strictly my fault.
- My family, who tolerates this writing habit of mine.
- The Mankato West High School Speech Team, which long ago tolerated my presence on the team and was the spark of inspiration for this story.

Discussion Guide

1. What made Jolia feel the way she did at the beginning of the book? How did these feelings impact her behavior? How did Jolia evolve from the beginning of the book to the end?

2. Why do you think Jolia is so reluctant to tell Caro she's failing speech? What influence did Caro have on Jolia. Was Caro a leader or follower? At the start of the story, do you think Caro pays too much attention to Jeremy at the expense of her relationship with Jolia? Do you think Jolia should have made her feelings known earlier?

3. What role did Tori play in the story, and how did she interact with Jolia? Why do you think Tori is so bossy? Why does Tori dislike Sam so much?

4. At the second tournament, Jolia must perform her selection in front of Sam. Later, she reflects that it's worse to fail in front of someone you know (rather than a group of strangers). Why does she feel this way? Do you agree with her? How did Sam help Jolia? What

strategies did he use to help Jolia overcome her fears? If you were Jolia, would you take Sam up on his offer of secret coaching?

5. Glossophobia is speech anxiety or the fear of public speaking. It's so prevalent that the Mayo Clinic devotes a page on its website to overcoming this fear. Why is public speaking such a scary thing? Is it one you have? Would you (or have you) tried some of the things Jolia does to overcome her fear?

6. The "tagline" for the novel is: Sometimes staying silent is the biggest lie of all. Several characters in the story have a secret or something they're hiding from someone else. Do you think not speaking up can be the same or even worse than lying? Why is it so hard to speak up, even when we know we should?

Special thanks to Laura Murphy and her mother/daughter book club, who inspired the creation of this reader guide and supplied several of the questions.

The Geek Girl's Guide to Cheerleading

Read the book VOYA calls contemporary, laugh-outloud funny, and positive.

When self-proclaimed geek girl Bethany Reynolds becomes the newest member of the varsity cheerleading squad, she realizes that there's one thing worse than blending into the lockers: getting noticed. Who knew cheerleading was so hard? Well, at least there's a manual, The Prairie Stone High Varsity Cheerleading Guide. Too bad it doesn't cover any of the really tough questions. Like:

- How do you maintain some semblance of dignity while wearing an insanely short skirt?
- What do you do when the head cheerleader spills her beer on you at your first in-crowd party?
- And how do you protect your best friend from the biggest player in the senior class?

Bethany is going to need all her geek brainpower just to survive the season!

The Fine Art of Holding Your Breath

MacKenna's mother died when she was a baby, a casualty of the first Gulf War. Now seventeen, MacKenna has spent her life navigating the minefield of her dad's moods, certain of one thing: she is destined to follow in her mother's combat boots. But when she pursues an ROTC scholarship, she finds herself at war before even enlisting.

Her father forbids her from joining the military, inexplicable considering he'd raised her to be a "warrior princess." MacKenna turns to her grandmother—who arms her with an ammo crate containing her mother's personal effects from the war. Hidden in the crate's false bottom is a journal, one her mom stashed there hours before her death.

While MacKenna untangles the secrets of her parents' tragic love story, her own life unravels. Dad's behavior becomes erratic, her best friend grows distant and even hostile, and a boy from her past returns—with a life-threatening secret of his own.

If ever a girl needed her mother, it's now.

The pen might be mightier than the sword, but are a mother's words strong enough to slice through years of hidden pain? Can those words reach through the battlefields of the past to change MacKenna's future?

Also by Charity Tahmaseb

YOUNG ADULT FICTION (WITH DARCY VANCE)

The Geek Girl's Guide to Cheerleading

Dating on the Dork Side

YOUNG ADULT FICTION

The Fine Art of Keeping Quiet

The Fine Art of Holding Your Breath

Now and Later: Eight Young Adult Short Stories

FANTASY

Coffee and Ghosts, Season 1: Must Love Ghosts

Coffee and Ghosts, Season 2: The Ghost That Got Away

Coffee and Ghosts, Season 3: Nothing but the Ghosts

Straying from the Path, Stories from the Sour Magic Series of Fairy Tales

About the Author

Charity Tahmaseb has slung corn on the cob for Green Giant and jumped out of airplanes (but not at the same time). She spent twelve years as a Girl Scout and six in the Army; that she wore a green uniform for both may not be a coincidence. These days, she writes fiction (long and short) and works as a technical writer for a software company in St. Paul.

Her novel, The *Geek Girl's Guide to Cheerleading* (written with co-author Darcy Vance), was a YALSA 2012 Popular Paperback pick in the Get Your Geek On category.

Her short speculative fiction has appeared in UFO Publishing's *Unidentified Funny Objects* and *Coffee* anthologies, *Flash Fiction Online*, and *Cicada*.

www.ingramcontent.com/pod-product-compliance
Lightning Source LLC
Chambersburg PA
CBHW031247120726
47905CB00002B/750